From Hollywood To Gettysburg

Copyright 2015 Craig Rupp

All rights reserved. No portion of this book may be reproduced in any form or by any means without explicit written permission from the author.

This book is dedicated to my family, friends, and all the hopeless romantics out there.

1

As her plane descended toward its landing in Harrisburg, PA, Katie Chambers sat quietly in her seat, staring at the beautiful sunrise taking place outside her window. Her boyfriend, Tommy Blake sat next to her reading a magazine. The Harrisburg, Pennsylvania Airport was just another layover stop on their countrywide movie premiere tour. Tommy and Katie were Hollywood's sweethearts. They had it all. Fame and fortune. Everyone loved them. Their movies were always a sure thing and every producer and director wanted them. This particular trip was for Tommy's latest film and they were on their way to Baltimore for a private screening with a few lucky contest winners.

"Katie! Katie! You ready to go?" Tommy asked.

Katie was so deeply consumed in thought she had no idea the plane had landed and everyone had already started to depart. "Yes, I'm ready, let's go," she replied.

Tommy Blake was your typical male Hollywood star. Long, dark wavy hair, a scruffy beard, jeans, tee shirt and five-hundred-dollar dress shoes. Katie Chambers too, was a typical female Hollywood star. Perfect blonde hair, designer jeans, thousand-dollar leather jacket and heels, and surprisingly, as they walked through the airport to catch their next flight, only a few people noticed who they were and respectfully, discreetly asked for autographs or "selfies" with them, but nobody really noticed them. This was after all, Harrisburg, Pennsylvania and not Los Angeles, California. After approaching their ticket counter, they heard the news most airport travelers dread to hear.

"I'm so sorry but your flight has been delayed," said the ticket agent behind the counter.

"Delayed? How long?" a seemingly angered and spoiled Tommy quipped.

"Right now, we're looking at four hours sir."

Tommy shook his head in disgust. Katie stood silently and closed her eyes.

"Aren't we near Baltimore? How long would it take me to drive there?" Tommy asked the ticket agent.

"About two hours sir," she said.

"Perfect, where's your nearest car rental place?" asked Tommy.

"You can find those on level one sir."

With that, Tommy and Katie found themselves walking through the airport towards level one to find a car and drive themselves to Baltimore. This was the last thing Katie wanted to have happen. The pair held a secret that no one knew of except them. They may be "Hollywood's sweethearts" in public. But when alone, they found it miserable to be around each other. When in private, they often had a civil discussion about why they hadn't broken up by now. Was it the money? The fear of losing fame? The fear of losing lead roles in movies? Fear of losing friends? They let their fear control their happiness and when they were alone with each other it was a sympathetic sight to see.

At the rental car counter the agent gave them a few brochures of things to do and see between Harrisburg and Baltimore. As they waited for the paperwork to be finished, Tommy sifted through the small stack of brochures and stopped.

"Gettysburg is on the way? Seriously? I've always wanted to see that place!" he said with excitement in his voice.

"Oh yes sir, it's about an hour or so from here," said the rental agent.

Tommy looked at Katie with a smile. She knew that smile all too well and her heart sank.

"Great, that means more time alone with him," she thought to herself. Now, she was dreading this trip even more.

2

As they drove down Route Fifteen south, Tommy was the first to notice one of the six Gettysburg exit signs.

"Yes," he said out loud.

"Can't we just keep going?" asked Katie.

She knew it would fall on deaf ears as Tommy kept to his plans. As they drove towards town, Katie was miserable. She wanted to be anywhere else right now, and with anybody else for that matter.

"Are you hungry? You want to grab a bite to eat?" asked Tommy.

Katie quietly stared out the passenger side window. Tommy knew she was upset but really didn't care.

"Let's check this place out," he said as they pulled into the National Park's Visitor Center. It was a semi-warm, sunny day out. Being celebrities, they were most of the time getting noticed by fans so sunny days and sunglasses sometimes helped conceal who they were. After all, they were now in Gettysburg, Pennsylvania not Los Angeles, California.

Tommy grew more and more excited as they approached the Visitor's Center and noticed a statue of Abraham Lincoln sitting on a bench to his left. He wanted to get a photo with Abe but knew better than to ask Katie to take it so he continued on and led her into the building. Once inside, Tommy asked Katie if there was anything she wanted to see.

"I just want to get to Baltimore so do what you need to do and let's get out of here," she said to him.

With her words, he left in a huff. For the first time, a slight smile appeared on her face. She knew she'd finally gotten to him.

Katie stood alone at the entrance of the Visitor's Center watching tourists walk by her without a clue of who she was. For the first time all day she felt at ease. She was alone. Nobody knew who she was and she could be herself for a change. She walked into the gift shop to take a look around. It was filled with anything you could want that was stamped with the name "Gettysburg." Shirts, hats, fake money, replica guns, CD's, DVD's, and books, lots and lots of books. Katie enjoyed to read. She didn't get much time to read, but she always liked getting lost in a good book. As she stood and looked through the different stacks and shelves full of books, one book in particular caught her eye. It was a book of photos taken in and around Gettysburg. She picked up the book and skimmed through the pages.

This is actually a beautiful place, she thought to herself.

She takes the book to the checkout counter and asks about the artist who had taken the photos.

"Oh my yes, this is Evan Walker's book," said the little old lady behind the counter. "He is one of our local residents that writes stories and takes lovely photos as well. You can find a few of his books in the corner over there," she added.

Katie walked to the corner that the woman pointed to. There she found some of Evan Walker's books. She picked up one titled "Love from Beyond" and started to read bits and pieces. It only took a few words but she knew she had to have this book. Katie takes the two books back to the counter to pay for them.

"Did you find everything you need dear?" asked the clerk.

"I sure did, thank you so much," said Katie.

The woman behind the counter gives Katie a puzzled look.

Uh-oh, here it comes, she recognizes me, Katie thought to herself.

The little old woman looks around as if to tell a secret, then looks at Katie.

"If you like his work, go into town dear. He's also a paranormal investigator and has written some spooky books about the ghosts around town, but we don't dare sell them here," she said.

"Really?" said Katie. "I will do just that, thanks," she said as she paid for her books and leaves the gift shop.

She sits on a bench near the large open windows and waits for Tommy. She takes the books out of bag and starts to skim through the pages once again. As she looked, she stopped to gaze at a page with a particularly beautiful photograph and was startled by a tap on the shoulder. She jumped.

"I'm so sorry," said a teenaged girl who was now standing in front of her. "Did anyone ever tell you that you look like Katie Chambers?"

Katie chuckled with relief. "Yes, I hear that from time to time."

"Well, I don't want to bother you but just wanted to tell you that. Enjoy your visit to Gettysburg," said the teenager.

"I will, thank you so much," said Katie. *Wow, not only is this town beautiful but the people here are very friendly too,* she thought.

After perusing the book of photos, Katie picked up her new copy of "Love from Beyond" and looked it over. She turned the book over to the back cover and for the first time saw Evan's photo along with a brief personal profile.

It was at that moment she knew why she was drawn to his books. Katie knew that somehow, someway, she had to meet this guy.

Katie looked up from her book to notice an old woman looking at her. Smiling. Katie smiled back and returned to her book.

Flipping through the pages, Katie heard a familiar voice coming up behind her.

"Okay, I've seen enough, are you ready to go to Baltimore?" asked Tommy.

She had to think quickly. "Can we go into town for a bit? I'm hungry and I heard they have some quaint little shops in town I'd like to see," she said to Tommy.

"Sure, why not? Let's go," he said.

They walked through the parking lot towards their rental car. Katie, for the first time in a long time, found her heart racing, excited to hopefully somehow run into her mystery guy.

As they drove into town looking for a place to eat Katie couldn't help notice the numerous shops along the streets. She noticed a shop that had books in the window.

"Park here," she said to Tommy.

Katie and Tommy got out of their car and looked around for a minute. Tommy saw a small restaurant and asked Katie if it looked okay to her.

"It's fine. Get us a table and I'll be right there, I want to check out this gift shop," she said to him.

Tommy walked to the restaurant as Katie walked to the souvenir shop. Once inside she was greeted by the girl behind the counter.

"Hello and welcome! If there's anything I can help you with just let me know."

"Actually, there is. Do you have any books by Evan Walker?" Katie asked.

"Oh yes, they're in the other room. You can't miss them," said the store clerk.

"Thank you," said Katie. As she walked to the other room the girl behind the counter watched her intently.

"Excuse me, but aren't you?" she asked.

"Yes, I am," said Katie with a smile. The girls face lit up with excitement. *How often do you have a celebrity of her stature walk into your little gift shop?*

Katie entered the room to look for the books. There were many, many filling the room. The girl who was behind the counter only seconds ago rushed to help her.

"Ummmmmm right over here, Miss Chambers," said the clerk.

There were four different books by Evan Walker but she didn't care. "I'll take one of each," said Katie.

"Wow, you sure are a fan of his work. Do you know him?" asked the store clerk.

"Actually, I was going to ask if you by chance know him," said Katie with a chuckle.

"I've never met him personally, but he does book signings around town sometimes," said the girl. "I heard he lives just outside of town along Route 30 but pretty much keeps to himself," she added.

As she stood at the register to pay for her books the girl behind the counter asked if she could get an autograph and a "selfie" with Katie.

"Sure," she replied.

"Thank you SO much Miss Chambers. Nobody will believe me when I tell them you stopped by here today," said the clerk.

"You're very welcome, but could you do me a favor and don't tell anyone, or post that on social media for a couple of days after I'm gone," Katie asked, as she signed her autograph on a piece of paper before leaving the store to meet up with Tommy.

Walking towards the restaurant, Katie couldn't help but notice how joyful everyone was. Families spending time together, couples holding hands, they all looked happy to be there. While looking around she saw her. The old woman from the visitor's center was standing across the street, all alone, again smiling at her. Katie doesn't smile back this time. The old woman suddenly gives her chills. She looks away and enters the restaurant.

Once inside, she spotted Tommy sitting at a booth.

"What the hell took so long?" Tommy sneered at her as she sat across from him.

"Shopping. There's so much to look at here, oh, and for the second time today I saw the same old lady staring at me. Kind of gives me the creeps" she said.

"Probably just a fan. What's in the bag?" asked Tommy.

"Just some books," she said.

"Let me see," he said as he grabs the bag off the table.

He takes the books out of the bag and looks at them. He laughs out loud, as if to embarrass her. "Ghosts?" Ghosts?" You bought books of ghost stories from around here? You were always into that stupid shit weren't you?" he said still laughing.

"Give me the car keys," she growled.

"What for?"

"Because you're an asshole and I'm done with all of this. I'm taking my bag and you can go to Baltimore without me. I'm staying here," she snapped.

"You're not serious?"

Katie didn't have to say a word, her glare said it all.

"Whatever!" he said as they left the table, paid the bill and returned to the car.

Back at the car, Katie opened the trunk and grabbed her suitcase.

"I thought you hated this place; like you're really going to stay here," Tommy said matter of factly.

Katie said nothing, but simply walked towards the crowded street, looking for the nearest hotel.

Tommy stood there, shaking his head as he watched her disappear into the crowds of tourists that were already walking up and down the streets of Gettysburg. He thought for just a second about going after her but somewhere in that moment his true feelings came out. Their relationship was a sham. He knew it. She knew it, and suddenly he didn't care what the public thought, so what if news of their breakup hit the tabloid papers. He felt a true to self-peaceful calm, then got in his car and drove towards Baltimore.

3

As Katie walked the streets searching for the right hotel she couldn't help but notice all the "Ghost Tours" signs that seemed to be on every street corner.

Wow, either this place is truly haunted like they say it is or there are a lot of people that are full of shit trying to make a quick sleazy buck off the paranormal world, she thought. Her thoughts were disrupted by the sound of a car pulling up beside her and a familiar voice she thought she'd heard the last of. It was Tommy, who drove back to give her one last chance.

"Katie, you're acting like a baby, get in the damn car," he said.

"Leave me alone!"

"Katie, I'm not going to tell you again! Get in the car now or I'm leaving you here!"

"Wrong! I'm leaving you! Bye!"

Angered by her words Tommy squeals the tires and drives away for good.

Finally, almost out of town she spots what looks like the perfect hotel for her. She walked in the front door and up to the desk to check in.

"Hello, do you have any rooms available?" she asked the clerk.

"Anything specific you were looking for?"

"Queen size would be fine," Katie replied.

"And for how long?"

"One week please." Katie spoke as the employee typed on the keyboard.

"You're in luck, yes we do." The clerk looked up from the computer screen.

"Great," Katie said with excitement.

"I'll need to see your I.D. and a form of payment," said the woman behind the counter. Katie handed the clerk her driver's license and credit card. As she looked at the card, the employee's eyes widened. She looked up from the driver's license back to Katie.

"Oh my God, I thought you looked like *her* but wasn't going to say anything. I mean, this is Gettysburg, the last place I would expect to see you," said the over excited clerk.

Katie chuckled and gave her one of those goofy, 'here I am, it's really me' faces.

"Could I ask a favor?" said Katie.

"Anything Miss Chambers, anything!"

"Could you please tell no one I'm in town? I'm here for a getaway and wouldn't want word out that I'm here," said Katie.

"Absolutely, I'll make a note in the computer so the other clerks won't say anything as well," she said.

"Thank you so much," said Katie.

After finishing checking in, the clerk asked if there was anything else she could do to make her stay more comfortable.

"As a matter of fact, there is. Do you have a blank piece of paper?" Katie asked.

"Sure do!" The desk employee handed her the paper.

"What is your name?" asked Katie.

"Jennifer."

With that Katie started to write on the blank piece of paper that lay in front of her. When she was done, she smiled at the woman, handed her the paper and left to go to her room.

The clerk looked at the piece of paper Katie just handed to her and read it. "To Jennifer! It was so very nice to meet you, thanks for all your help! Katie Chambers."

Katie found her room, unlocked the door with her keycard and went inside. In the room, with the door closed, she grabbed her books and laid on the bed to look over them once again. She skimmed through the pages of each book, stopping from time to time so she could look at Evan Walker's photo on the back cover. Finally, as she grew weary and tired, she grabbed the book of photos and fell fast asleep.

4

Katie awoke, dazed and confused. She had forgotten where she was. She looked at her watch. It read four thirty-five a.m. A glance at the books spread out all over the bed quickly jogged her memory of where she was and why.

"Perhaps since I'm up early I'll be lucky enough to see one of those beautiful sunrises pictured in the book," she said to herself. She started the coffeemaker, grabbed her make up bag and went into the bathroom to take a shower.

Showered, dressed, and with a bit of makeup dabbled on, Katie sat on the bed sipping a cup of coffee and looking through the book of photography. She checked an app on her phone that told her when the sun rises and sets, then looked at her watch. She had about twenty minutes to walk out to the battlefields, only a short distance from her hotel. Katie grabbed her book of photos, keycard, cell phone, sunglasses and walked out the door towards the battlefields. She stopped and paused for a moment, then looked towards the deep blue early morning sky.

"God, I know I don't talk to you as much as I should. And I honestly don't know why I suddenly find myself here of all places. Is there someone I'm supposed to meet? If so, could you give me a sign? Or lead me in the right direction? Thank you."

Even for someone like Katie, who knew nothing about the Battle of Gettysburg, it wasn't hard to figure out where the battlefields were. There were cannons and monuments everywhere, each marking a historic, specific location. With a group of cannons in sight that's exactly where Katie's instincts led her.

As she walked towards her destination, Katie couldn't help but notice that there was nobody else out and about. An occasional car passed by, but compared to the large crowds of yesterday, the place seemed like it had been deserted. Finally arriving at the spot she had chosen, it was clear to Katie that this morning's sunrise was going to be a beautiful one. She took her phone from her pocket and started to take photos, moving from one location to another and stooping for different angles while doing so. As she walked up a small hill she noticed an SUV parked on the side of the road. Katie looked, but didn't see anyone around. *Maybe they're just out for a walk this morning,* she thought while walking towards the SUV, stopping to take a photo every now and then.

As she walked by the SUV, lost in her own little world, Katie was startled by movement. A man stood with his camera and tripod taking photos just as she was. He had his back to her so he didn't see her jump.

"Good morning," she said to the man.

Now the tables were turned. He had not seen her behind him. With her words, he swung around, quite surprised.

"Uhhhh, good morning to you too," the man said to Katie. "Beautiful day for photos, isn't it?" he added.

Katie said nothing. As soon as the man had turned around she knew exactly who he was. She instantly recognized that face. Her heartbeat quickened. The light brown hair, blue eyes were easy. What she didn't expect was seeing such an athletic body.

"Evan?" she asked.

Once again, the man looked surprised. He had no idea who this woman was, but she knew his name.

"Yes, but I'm sorry, do I know you?" he asked.

So much was zipping through her mind all at once. She wasn't exactly sure what to say.

"No, you don't know me, but I purchased a few of your books in town yesterday," she said with a nervous laugh.

"Oh, well thank you, you're now one of the six people who have actually bought my books," he said with a laugh.

His words made her laugh along with him and suddenly her nervousness went away.

"This is the best time to be out here, no cars, and no tourists getting in the way. I find it very peaceful so you picked a great time to be out here as well," Evan said to her.

"Beginners luck," she joked.

"What made you come out here so early…..I'm sorry, I didn't get your name," Evan said with a pause.

Katie panicked. For some strange reason, she didn't want him to know who she really was. Staring at the beautiful sunrise only one name came quickly to mind.

"Dawn, my name is Dawn. And truth be told, your photos made me come out here," she added.

"Well, it's very nice to meet you Dawn, and I'm honored, thank you," said Evan.

"Welcome," she said.

"I also hear you're into ghost hunting, which must be exciting," said Katie.

Evan laughed. "It has its moments."

"I love to watch the ghost hunting TV shows. They always make it exciting," said Katie.

Once again Evan laughed, only louder this time. "Well, let's just say, don't get caught up in the TV shows.

Most of it is fake and edited you know. It's entertainment," he said.

"No way!"

"Yeah way, and I'm not just saying that. I know people that have been on location when they filmed. I hear things from good resources," Evan said with a laugh. "In reality, sometimes nothing happens at all and that's just the way it goes," he added.

"Well, you just opened my eyes," said Katie with a laugh.

"People need to know the difference between truth and entertainment," he added.

As they stood and talked they both looked at the sun and realized it was now high in the sky. This morning's sunrise photo session was no longer an option.

"I'm so sorry. I've been talking and ruined your photo time," said Katie.

"Meh, I've got thousands of photos, so it's all good," said Evan with a smile.

His smile made Katie smile even bigger.

"Could I make it up to you by buying breakfast?" she asked.

"You know, that actually sounds very nice, thank you," said Evan. He packed up his camera equipment and threw it in the back as they climbed into his SUV.

"Any place special you'd like to go?" asked Evan.

"I'll trust you to make that decision," said Katie with a chuckle.

Evan drove them to a diner on the other side of town.

"Great food here, plus the best cheesecake in town if you're interested," said Evan.

They parked and walked across the street to the diner. Evan held the door open and then followed Katie into the diner.

"Good morning Evan, seat yourselves," said one of the waitresses as she grabbed two menus from behind the counter.

"Thank you Rose," said Evan as he led Katie towards a quiet window booth.

"Can I start you two out with some….coffee," Rose asked, as she handed them their menus. She stared at Katie.

Shit, don't say it, Katie thought to herself. But it was too late.

"Aren't you that actress?" asked Rose. "Ohhh my mind is terrible these days. What's her name? Katie, Katie…..Chambers," she finally said proudly.

Katie was now terrified. This waitress could blow her cover. She stared back, speechless.

"Rose, this is my friend Dawn," said Evan with a laugh.

"Nice to meet you Dawn and you do look like that actress, I'm just saying," laughed Rose. With those words, all three laughed together and quickly brought ease to Katie.

"I hear that a lot," Katie laughed.

Rose poured their coffee and told them she'd be back in a few minutes to get their orders.

"You know, I watch a lot of movies, and yea, she's right, you do kind of resemble that Katie Chambers girl now that I look at you," said Evan with a laugh.

"I wish I had her money," Katie shot back, faking a hearty laugh.

Katie decides the waitresses' questions were too close to call. She starts asking Evan questions about himself and the town, diverting the attention away from herself.

"So how long have you lived here Evan?"

"I've only lived here about three years. Before that I lived up north about three hours from here. I used to drive to Gettysburg like, once a month."

"Three hours once a month, really?"

"Right? Sometimes twice a month. This town, I don't know, there's just something magical about it. It draws me in, like I'm supposed to be here. Sounds crazy right?"

"No, I think I'm starting to get it. Is there a particular place here that you would say is the most haunted?"

"There's an inn, a few miles outside of town that I would have to say is the most haunted."

"Yea? So, you've had personal experiences there?"

"Many!"

"Can you tell me some or do I have to read your books," asked a smiling Katie.

"Actually, the best places aren't in any of my books. See, once a place gets out then it becomes over crowded with wannabee TV ghost hunters and some are very rude. Very disrespectful. I'll be straight up, I can't stand those types of people so I keep my favorite places to myself or the few close friends I have. I'll share with them."

"Fair enough. Tell me about your photos. What inspires you?"

"The beauty of the area I guess I'd have to say. I try to combine both the history and the beauty nature provides."

"I'm sorry, other than the Gettysburg Address, which I had to learn in school, I really don't know what happened here."

"This is hallowed ground. Some say the Battle of Gettysburg was the turning point of the Civil War, even though it lasted for another two years. The confederate army under General Lee basically got wiped out by General Meade and the union forces here. There were over fifty-two thousand casualties from both sides in just three days."

"Fifty-two thousand? That's horrible!"

"There are supposedly still hundreds of bodies still buried in the yards and fields in and around town."

"That's so sad. Nobody came to get them?"

"They may have come. By the time many came up with the means to get here the grave markers, usually planks of wood stuck in the ground were gone so they had no idea where their loved ones were buried."

"Oh my gosh, that makes me want to cry for them."

"See, this town does that to you."

"So, where are some of your favorite places on the battlefield? You must have a few?"

"I have some favorites. Spangler's Spring, Little Round Top and Devil's Den are a few."

"Little Round Top? What's that?"

"It was made famous by colonel Joshua Chamberlain and his bayonet charge against the confederates that were trying to gain the high ground on the second day. It's a spot with a beautiful view of the battlefield and a great place for sunset photos."

"I'll have to remember that."

"You don't want to visit without going there. You'll regret it."

"So, what else would you recommend seeing and doing while I'm in town?"

"Oh man, she puts me on the spot!"

"The spot," Katie said with a chuckle.

"Yeah, there's so much here. I don't think I've seen everything yet," he said laughing.

Evan glances at his watch. A smile disappears with a new look of disappointment.

"Well thank you for breakfast Dawn. I hate to cut this short but I've got to get to a doctor's appointment. Where can I drop you off?" asked Evan.

Her heart sank. It seemed crazy but she wanted to spend as much time as possible with this guy, even though she barely knew him. Deep inside she wanted to know everything about him.

"I'm staying at the hotel near the end of town, where we first met this morning."

Evan knew exactly where that was. Before he moved here, it was his favorite hotel to stay at when visiting.

"You have good taste, that's my favorite hotel," he said to her.

"Here's a little secret." His eyes had a mysterious glint. It's haunted, so keep your eyes and ears open," he added.

"Really?" Katie could hear the excitement in her own voice.

"Oh yeah, I have a few stories," said Evan with a chuckle as he pulled into the hotel parking lot.

"I don't mean to sound forward, but are you doing anything later?" asked Katie. "Would you have time to take me on a real live ghost hunt?"

"Sure, I think we can make that happen. But first, how would you like to see the area? Do some touristy things?"

"Now I'm intrigued, what did you have in mind?"

"Ever ridden a horse? Or a Segway?"

"They have those here?"

"Oh yea. They can make your tour very interesting. Especially the horses," Evan said with a laugh.

"Believe it or not I've never been on a horse."

"For real?"

"Hey, I'm from the city," Katie laughed.

"Well hell then, as soon as I'm done with my appointment I'm getting you on a horse. I'll make the arrangements and see you back here in about an hour or so. Sound good?"

"Sounds great!"

Evan pulls out of the parking lot and disappears into the traffic. Katie walks across the street to pass the time browsing the souvenir shops. She walks back to the hotel and arrives at almost the same time Evan pulls in the parking lot.

"Hey you," Katie says with a grin.

"Hi Dawn! You ready to ride a horse? I've got it all set up with a friend of mine."

"You're kidding? You're not kidding! I didn't think you were serious."

"Hey, don't ever doubt anything I say young lady," Evan laughed.

Katie jumps in Evan's SUV. They drive to the edge of town where his friend owns a horse tour company. They exit the truck and walk to the barn where Evan's friend Matt is waiting for them.

"Matty, how are you man? Thanks for doing this. Matty this is Dawn, Dawn this is Matt. Or Matty as we call him."

"Hi Matt, it's nice to meet you."

"Dawn, it's nice to meet you too. So, I have to ask, how did this guy talk a pretty girl like you into riding a horse?"

"Watch this guy," Evan laughed.

"I'm honestly still trying to figure this one out. I guess he just has a way with words."

"That he does my dear, that he does," Matt said as he led Evan and Katie to their horses. Katie's was brown and white; Evan's all black.

"Katie this will be yours," said Matt.

"What a beautiful horse," she said.

"They're both quarter horses but some call yours a paint horse because of the colors. Her name is Adaline and she'll take good care of you. Evan, yours is Ole Blackie."

Matt and Evan help Katie onto Adaline before Evan hops onto his horse.

"It's been awhile since you've been here Evan. Still remember your way around," asked Matt.

"I'm pretty sure I know where to go."

"Just stay on the trails I've got marked and when you get into the park just be careful crossing the roads. You know these tourists, looking at everything but the roads. They never pay attention."

"Dude, we'll be fine. I know all about the tourists, trust me. I got this," Evan laughed.

"Okay, okay!"

"Matt, should I be worried," asked Katie with a laugh.

"He says he's got this so you're in his hands now. God be with you."

"If I'm in his hands then I think everything will be just fine," she said looking towards Evan with a smile.

Matt gives Katie some quick instructions on how to control the reins before the two ride off.

"We shall return Matty," said Evan.

"Be safe and have fun."

5

Evan and Katie ride side by side through the woods and farmland. Katie quickly learns how to control her horse and is riding like a pro in no time.

"If someone told me I'd be riding a horse in the Pennsylvania woods I would've told them they were crazy. I love this. What a beautiful animal. So calm, not at all what I expected."

"You're doing great; are you sure you've never ridden a horse before?"

"I'm glad you talked me into this Evan. You're getting me outside my comfort zone. It's been awhile."

"Comfort zone?"

"I don't like to go out much. I never get any privacy. People are always…."

Katie quickly realizes she's talking about her celebrity life and the paparazzi that follow her everywhere. She quickly stops talking, again fearing not to blow her cover.

"Always," asks Evan.

"Huh?"

"You said people are always, then you stopped."

"Oh that. Yea, you know. People always seem to be in your business. You have to be careful these days. Too many fake friends out there. Gossipers. I'd rather just keep to myself."

"Makes sense, especially with all the social media out there. People say I'm stuck up or think I think I'm too good because I'm quiet and keep to myself. I totally get it."

"People can be so rude, right?"

"Right. And it all goes back to too many assumptions. And speaking of assumptions, I assume if we stop for a rest you'll be able to get back on your horse?"

"Oh, I think I can manage," Katie said with a smile.

"Are we stopping now?"

"Not yet, just around this corner."

Evan and Katie ride around the corner. A beautiful old farmhouse and barn majestically appear. Evan gets off his horse then helps Katie off hers.

"Oh, my God Evan. This place is absolutely gorgeous!"

"It is right? You can barely see it from the road so this is the only way to truly appreciate it."

"Who owns this place, I may just have to buy it."

"Ha! I don't know how much they'd want but I'm sure it's a price neither one of us could afford."

"Price wouldn't be a...."

Once again Katie catches herself and stops talking abruptly. Evan looks at her inquisitively.

"Price wouldn't be a," he asks.

"Huh?"

"You said the price wouldn't be a, then stopped."

"Oh, yeah, just dreaming of one of those, if I hit the lottery moments," she said with a laugh.

"Been there. Do that all the time myself," said Evan as they both laughed.

"Back to reality, who does own this place," Katie asked.

"I'm not sure to be honest with you. The park service most likely, unless it's been handed down through the family over time. This place was here at the time of the battle. Have you ever heard of Pickett's Charge?"

"Pickett's what?"

"That's what I thought," Evan chuckled.

Evan points to different locations as he explains a summary of Pickett's Charge.

July third was the last day of the Battle of Gettysburg. Behind you was the confederate lines. About fifteen thousand men left those woods and headed towards that clump of trees over there, also known as the high-water mark, where about seven thousand union soldiers were waiting for them.

"What happened?"

"Putting it mildly, after a barrage of cannon fire from both sides, the confederates left the safety of the woods and marched across these very fields to attack. Thousands of men didn't survive. Never made it. Look down at your feet. Chances are, someone died on that very spot," Evan explained.

"That's so sad. It's horrible."

"That's war. Nothing good ever comes of it."

"It's so beautiful here. It's hard to imagine what this was like during that time."

"That's why they call this hallowed ground. So many lost their lives here; and some, still remain here."

"That is heartbreaking."

"Okay young lady, that's your history lesson for today, let's continue on and I promise not to bring up death anymore. Keeping it real, keeping it positive."

"It's all very interesting. I don't mind learning this way. Death is part of what happened here and that's the reality, so it's okay to talk about it. It moves me."

"Nah, death is all too real. This is a happy time. So, tell me a little more about yourself Dawn."

Katie's heart starts to pound. She's caught off guard with his question. She's never been to Baltimore and has no idea what to say. She talks fast and tries to change the subject quickly.

"Well, I live just outside of Baltimore. I live with my mother who's not doing well health wise so I take care of her."

"I'm sorry to hear that."

"Thank you, she's a strong woman. I'm in between jobs right now but we get by."

"Ever get to any baseball games?"

"Sorry, I'm not much of a fan."

"What? They have a beautiful stadium there. It's amazing!"

"I take it you're a baseball fan?"

"Ahhhh, I love baseball. It is America's game you know."

"So I've heard."

"Well, one of these days I might have to let you show me around Baltimore."

Knowing nothing about Baltimore, Katie quickly changes the subject.

"Your turn Evan, tell me more about you."

"Me?

"Yes you."

"You really want me to bore you to death while on this beautiful ride," he joked.

"There you go again, talking about death," Katie laughed.

"Oh shit, sorry!"

"See, you make me laugh so I would not call that boring."

Hmmm, let me think. Well, I told you I'm pretty quiet and, like you, I like to keep to myself. That's about it really."

"Come on, there's got to be more to Evan Walker than that. What are your likes? Your dislikes? Your hopes? Your dreams?

"Wow! Okay, let's see. I like writing and taking photos of course."

"Of course."

"I love playing golf, it's very relaxing if you're not too serious about it. I love the sunrises and the sunsets here. The beauty is something you just can't capture in a simple picture. I love hot fudge sundaes, hot coffee first thing in the morning, random road trips to anywhere for a day, a good romance movie, cuddling…."

"Cuddling? Did you just say cuddling," Katie asked surprised.

"Yes Dawn, it's true. I am a cuddler. But don't be getting any ideas, I'm not that easy."

"See, you are not boring. You sound like the perfect guy."

"Ha!"

"Okay, keep going. Your hopes? Your dreams?"

"Dislikes. Large crowds. People that drive like morons. Mean people I guess. They suck!"

"Hopes? Dreams?"

"Well, I had hoped to sell more than five books and you bought number six so, thank you, my dreams have come true."

"I haven't laughed this much in, I can't tell you how long."

"Oh, I'm sorry to hear that."

"See, there you go again," Katie said, still laughing.

Katie hasn't felt this kind of happiness in years. Her feelings take over. She leans in to kiss Evan. He backs away and looks towards the dark rain clouds heading their way.

"We should probably start riding back now. Looks like rain heading our way."

"Oh, okay. Ready when you are."

Evan helps Katie back onto her horse, mounts his and ride side by side back to the horse tour stables where they are greeted by Matt.

"I was getting worried about you two. Dawn, I see you survived."

"I survived. I was in good hands."

Hearing Katie's words, Matt gave Evan the, that a boy look.

"We stopped at the farm to rest a bit," Evan said.

"Well, I'm glad you're both back safely. Looks like rain coming our way, but who knows, the weather is crazy here sometimes."

"I noticed the skies. That's why we headed back. I owe you for this, thanks so much buddy."

"Oh I know, don't worry, I'll collect," Matt joked.

"Thank you for all of this Matt, it was very nice to meet you."

"You're very welcome Dawn. Anything for this guy. I'm glad you enjoyed yourselves. Come back anytime."

The trio say their good byes. Matt leads his horses back into the stables as Evan and Katie get into his SUV and drive back into town. Evan pulls into the parking space in front of Katie's room.

"I just realized something. Where is your car," Evan asks.

Once again Katie is caught off guard. She thinks fast.

"I came here with a friend. It was supposed to be a one day trip but I saw how amazing it was here, then came across your books and really saw how beautiful it was and decided to stay an extra few days. She went back home and said she'd pick me up when I was ready. So technically, it's your fault I'm still here."

"Okay, okay, sorry. Won't ask any more questions then," said Evan with a smile.

"So, what about that ghost hunting tour? Can you still show me around?"

"I think I have time later. I'm going to run home and grab a shower after sitting on that horse. Beautiful animals, but not so good on the nose."

"I was thinking the same thing. But I'll get my shower here of course."

"Alrighty then, I'll be back later. How does seven sound? Bring your camera, I know a great place for some killer sunset pictures while we're out."

"Are we going to this Little Round Top place you keep talking about?"

"Maybe. You'll just have to wait and see now won't you."

"Tease," Katie said with a smile.

"Tease?"

"I'm kidding. I can't wait until later."

"See you then Dawn."

Evan eases out of the parking lot into traffic. Katie watches him until he disappears into town then goes into her room. Katie shut the door and jumped onto her bed like an excited kid at Christmas time. She grabbed one of her books and started skimming through the ghost stories. She wanted to pick a few of the creepy places Evan had written about and see them for herself. She glanced at her watch and noticed she still had about four hours until Evan returned.

As she read through the book, Katie's eyes grew weary and before long she fell fast asleep.

Knock, knock, knock, knock!

Katie quickly sat up on her bed, in a confused state. *Where was she? What time was it? And who could be knocking on her door?*

She looked at her watch once again. It read five minutes after seven.

"Shit! I slept that long!" She scrambled towards the door. Katie embarrassingly opened the door.

"I'm so sorry, I must have fallen asleep," she said to Evan.

"I guess that's the reason why you have slobber all down your face then?" said Evan with a laugh.

"What?!" Horrified, Katie wiped her hands across her cheeks.

"I'm kidding!" Evan was still laughing. "C'mon, we'll get you some coffee and you'll be good as new in no time" he added.

The two hopped in Evan's SUV, stopped for coffee to go and were headed out to the battlefields. As they drove, Evan pointed out a few historical locations that had great meaning when it came to the civil war.

"Where are we going first?" asked Katie.

"The sun is about to go down so I'm going to take you to one of my favorite places."

"Little Round Top?"

"Nope!"

"Wait, what? No Little Round Top?"

"Maybe."

"Are you messing with me right now?"

"Uh, define messing with."

"Uh, I hate you right now, you know that right?"

"Good because I hate you right now too."

Something about Evan and Katie saying they hate each other make them laugh uncontrollably. Even though they just met, it's like they've been together forever.

Evan parks his SUV, grabs his camera bag and coffee then proceeds to open the door to help Katie out of the truck.

"Is this it?" Katie asks.

"Welcome to Little Round Top. I think you'll like it," he said with a smile.

Evan stayed behind Katie as they walked up the short path to Little Round Top. He knew all too well what would be waiting when they reached the top but wanted to see her reaction once they came to the opening. As they approached the top Katie stopped for a moment, then turned to Evan with a look of awe.

"Oh my God it's beautiful up here. No wonder this is one of your favorite places."

"Still hate me," he asks.

"I could never hate you. You are incredible."

"Whew, good because I never hated you either, just saying."

"Oh my God you are something else," Katie laughed.

"I thought you'd enjoy this. Follow me Dawn," he said as he took the lead. They walked past the statue of a man standing on a huge boulder holding binoculars and then followed a small dirt path that ran in front of the statue.

"Okay, sit your coffee down and let me help you up," Evan said to Katie as they now stood beside another huge boulder. She set her coffee down and Evan lifted her onto the rock. He then handed the coffee cups and his camera bag up to Katie and proceeded to climb up onto the rock to sit down next to her.

"Welcome to my favorite place Dawn. I love to sit on this rock and watch the sunset."

"You definitely have an amazing view from here."

"Did you happen to see the movie *Gettysburg* that was filmed here on location," he asked her.

Embarrassed, Katie covered her eyes and said, "Noooooo, I'm sorry."

Evan laughed. "Don't be sorry. It's not the kind of movie you girls would watch, but if you ever do, two of the films major stars sat right on this very rock in the movie."

"Well I'm sold! Now I'm going to have to watch it."

"It's three hours long but very well made. Also, really cool to see some of the places in the film come to life and then go to the very location with a visual of what happened during the battle. Yep, that's what we small town folk do for excitement around here."

"I'm starting to realize there's not one thing wrong with small town life," Katie said.

"Well, if you hit cow tipping stage, there's no coming back from that low point. There's good small town and bad small town."

Again, his comedic rhetoric and quick wit had Katie laughing and smiling.

"You're making my cheeks hurt. I haven't laughed this much in, my gosh, I can't remember how long."

"Oh, I'm sorry to hear that."

"See, there you go again. You're cracking me up."

"Damn, now I have to figure out a really great encore. No pressure there. Geez, thanks Dawn."

"Stop it," Katie said, tears of happiness trickling down her face.

"Okay, okay. But I will say this and remember it. You can't take life too seriously, you'll never get out alive."

"I think I've heard that somewhere before."

Katie wants to capture this moment in time so she grabs her phone and starts taking photos. Evan grabbed a camera from his bag, adjusted a few settings and started to snap a few photos as well.

"So, after this beautiful sunset, where are we going next?"

"Well, I have a few places I could show you, but I was going to ask you if there was anywhere particular you wanted to see," said Evan.

"I would love to see the location where you may or may not have seen the group of Confederate soldiers walking through the woods."

Evan looked surprised. "Well I see someone has been reading someone else's book," he said with a laugh.

"I told ya!" She joined in his laughter. In that moment, she realized her cheeks had really begun to hurt.

A good hurt. She hadn't smiled or laughed this much in a long, long time. It was, as they say, a good pain.

As the sun showed the last of its brilliant rays they sat in silence, taking in the moment. Without taking her eyes off the beautiful surroundings in front of her, Katie asked Evan to tell her a little bit more about himself.

"Hmmm, well you already know I enjoy writing and taking photographs," he said.

"Do you have family here?" she asked.

"No, no family anywhere. No kids, and my parents have passed away. I have a few cousins but don't really keep in touch."

For some reason this made Katie very sad and Evan could see it in her expression.

"Hey, none of that. This is a happy time right now so don't even go there. It is what it is," he said.

She gave him a smile. By now the sun had gone down and darkness was all but setting in.

"Are you ready to go see that spot now," Evan asked.

"Absolutely, let's do this."

He packed up his camera bag, jumped off the rock and proceeded to help Katie down. They both walked to his SUV for the drive to the other side of the park.

Driving through the twisty, curvy park roads at night, lit only by the headlights of Evan's SUV was creepy to Katie, but it also gave her a strange adrenaline rush. Evan pulled off on the side of the road and turned his lights off. Nerves twisted in her stomach. Evan then turned the lights back on.

"See that spot right over there? That is where I saw the group of Confederate soldiers marching one rainy evening," said Evan.

"Can we get out and walk around?" asked Katie.

Evan looked at the clock. It was nine-thirty. The park closed at ten.

"Sure, we have a few minutes but we have to be out of here by ten. Want to try for some EVP?" he asked.

"Yes!" said an excited Katie. *My first real try at EVP - how freakin' cool is this,* she thought as they walked through the dark, quiet woods.

"I'll let you ask all the questions if you want to," said Evan.

"What I should ask?"

"Normally I ask for a name, or state, if they are Union or Confederate, did they die here, the year, things like that," Evan explained.

Katie, having a good memory from remembering lines for her movies, asked each question in the order Evan had just suggested. When he played back the recorder you could hear Katie asking questions - but no answers. That is until she asked if there was anyone there that was Union or Confederate. On the audio, they clearly heard something say the word "Confederate!"

"Oh my God, oh my God did you hear that? Did you hear the word Confederate too?" screeched an excited Katie.

"I did hear that. Congratulations, they must really enjoy talking to you. You got an EVP on your very first time out. It took me a few tries so you're doing better than I did," Evan chuckled.

"Oh my God this is SO cool," she said. "Can we try again?"

Evan looked at his watch. They had five minutes to leave the park.

"I'm so sorry but we have to go."

"Shoot, okay," she said. She understood because she remembered one thing Evan had told her earlier. Always be respectful of the park, its rules, and especially to the spirits that still linger there. As they drove out of the park, they passed a Park Ranger truck.

"Whew, that was close," said Evan with a laugh, which in turn made Katie laugh. Once again, in the darkness of night she felt her cheeks hurting but didn't care. It was a good hurt after all.

Evan turned his SUV in the direction of Katie's hotel.

"I know you're probably busy and I don't mean to take up all of your free time but could we do something again tomorrow," asked Katie.

Evan laughed. "Trust me. You aren't taking up any of my time. I'm enjoying your company. But, I do have a couple of doctor appointments tomorrow so maybe we could get lunch in between?"

"Two doctor appointments, is everything okay," she asked.

Evan grew quiet for a moment.

"Evan?"

Evan looked at her and smiled.

"Yeah, everything is good. I'm just a hypochondriac," he said with a laugh. His words eased her worries a bit, but deep inside she felt things weren't what they seemed.

Evan pulled into the hotel parking lot and stopped in front of Katie's room.

"Can I see your phone for a second," she asked. Evan handed her his phone.

She clicked a few buttons and gave it back to him.

"There, now you have my number, text me when you're ready for lunch tomorrow," she said as she got out of his SUV.

"Deal, goodnight Dawn," he said with a smile.

"Goodnight Evan." She closed the door and walked to her room. She opened the door and stood there, watching Evan drive out of sight. She quickly closed the door and walked towards the office. She was hoping to see Jennifer behind the front desk. Katie held her breathe as she walked into the lobby and towards the desk. Nobody was there.

"Hello," she yelled out.

"One second" she heard a female voice call out to her. "I'm sorry how can I....Miss Chambers, it's so great to see you," said the voice.

To Katie's relief, it was Jennifer.

"What can I do for you?" asked the cute red-haired girl.

"Is there anywhere nearby I can rent a car," Katie asked.

"There is a place a few miles outside of town. You can't walk there and it's closed right now but I could give you a lift if you need one," said Jennifer.

"Shoot, thank you but that sounds like more trouble than it's worth. I only need it for a few hours," said Katie.

"When do you need it?" Jennifer's green eyes met Katie's.

"Tomorrow around two."

"Well, I'll be here working a double starting at noon so you're more than welcome to borrow my car if you'd like."

Katie's eyes widened. "Are you serious? That would be so nice of you," she said.

"Anytime."

Katie grabbed a piece of paper and asked Jennifer if she could have her number. She gladly gave it to her.

"I'll text you tomorrow when I need it. Thank you again!" Katie walked out of the office and back to her room. Once inside, she decided to take a shower before bed. As she stood under the hot running water, thinking about Evan and all the wonderful memories he had provided her today, it made her smile. She'd forgotten how good it felt to be happy.

6

Sunshine bled through the curtains, infiltrating the quiet room. She grabbed a pillow from the bed and stuck it over her head. As she lay there under the blankets and pillows she thought about Evan and wondered if he too was up this early. She rolled over and looked at the clock on the table. It read ten-thirty. Eyes that just a few seconds ago had squinted at the light now opened wider.

Ten-thirty, no freakin' way! She sat on the edge of the bed, deep in thought.

Who was this Evan guy and why after only one day did he have such a deep connection with her? She honestly did not believe in love. After all, she lived in Hollywood where everyone it seemed, was an actor, and no one could hold onto a marriage for longer than a heartbeat. This feeling she had was something that she could only describe as living in a fairytale movie.

She looked at the coffee pot sitting on the desk. It took her back to last evening when she and Evan were sitting on what he called his special rock, sharing coffee. Katie smiled. She arose from the bed and started a pot of the coffee and then went into the bathroom for another shower. She kept this one short as she also had to do her makeup and other things. She wanted to be ready when Evan sent her a text.

After showering, and doing her hair and makeup she looked at her watch which now read eleven forty-five. Almost as if on cue, her phone beeped.

'Be there in five,' read the text.

'Ok sounds good, all ready,' she texted back.

Katie grabbed her keys and purse then went outside to meet Evan. As he pulled into the parking lot she could see a big smile coming from behind the driver's side windshield. Evan pulled into the space in front of her room.

"Morning Dawn," he said as she climbed into the passenger seat.

"Good morning Evan, how are you? How did your appointment go?"

"I'm good thanks. A doctor appointment is a doctor appointment. Are any of them ever good," he asked with a chuckle.

"Ya got me there," laughed Katie.

"Are you in the mood for some Italian food," he asked.

"That sounds really good right about now."

"Italian it is then," he said with a smile.

They drove through town and parked in front of the little Italian restaurant. It wasn't busy yet and that's the way Evan liked it. They enter and a hostess seats them at a booth.

"Wow! This place is so cool!"

"Isn't it? I like how they fixed it up. Looks like you're really in Italy, doesn't it?"

"It does. Italy is amazing. The buildings are just naturally like this. Old looking I mean. They did a great job of making this place look authentic."

"Oh, you've been to Italy," Evan asks.

As careful as she's tried to be, Katie has just made her first major mistake and the bewildered look on Evan's face forces her to think fast.

"Never. But it's on my bucket list. I think I've watched every television show that explores the beauty and history of Italy. It looks like an amazing place. Have you ever been there," she asks.

"No, this is about as close as I'll ever come to being in Italy."

"Is it a place you'd like to see someday?"

"I would love to see Europe someday. But selling books isn't going to do it. Pretty sure anyway."

"Any country you have on your bucket list," asks Katie.

"Oh yea! Ireland! I'll probably sound like you but I think I've watched every single TV show about that place. It looks incredible. Maybe someday I'll get there."

"Think positive. You never know Evan."

"That's true. We have to try and be positive no matter what comes up in life."

"Are you trying to tell me something?"

"Nope, just keeping it real."

"Well, you're real, and I'm real. I'd say we're doing just that."

"Speaking of real, did anything strange happen in your hotel room last night?"

"To be honest with you, I slept like a baby, so if anything did happen I slept right through it," she laughed.

"Don't feel bad, my apartment is haunted and all was quiet at my place last night as well," he laughed.

"For real? Are you serious? Can I see it?" The words flew out of Katie's mouth so fast that even Evan looked stunned.

"Uhhhh, maybe, I guess so," he stammered.

Great, way to go stupid, now he probably thinks you're some kind of easy skank, she thought.

"Wait. How do I know you're not a serial killer or something," Evan joked.

His words brought quick relief and laughter to Katie. "I swear to you I am not," she laughed.

They ate their lunch and chatted and the time flew by, until Evan looked at his watch. "Damn, I gotta get going, it's almost time for my appointment."

"My paranoia is telling me you're trying to get rid of me," joked Katie.

"I swear Dawn, if I could keep this going I would. But…." he said with a pause.

"I was kidding silly. I understand."

As they drove back to Katie's hotel, she took her phone out and sent a 'could I use your car now?' text to Jennifer.

Beep. 'Come and get it' was the text she got back.

As Evan pulled his SUV into the hotel parking lot Katie asked him to drop her off at the office as she had to take care of something at the front desk.

"Will you be around later?" asked Katie.

Evan paused. "Um, maybe yea, I'll see how things go," he said.

"Great, hope to hear from you." She smiled, suddenly feeling shy.

"Dawn, enjoy your day," said Evan.

"Thank you, I will. See you later," she said as she got out of his truck and started towards the office. Once inside she ran over to Jennifer who handed her the keys.

"It's the blue one sitting right out there," said Jennifer, pointing toward the corner of the lot.

"Thank you, thank you, thank you," said Katie as she ran for the car, hoping to catch up to Evan. She pulled onto the street and as luck would have it, Evan was stuck at a red light. She was four cars behind him. That was perfect. Hopefully he wouldn't notice her. She followed him through town and then the outskirts of town. Her mind started to get the best of her.

Is he married? A girlfriend? Just trying to get rid of me? Am I being too pushy? Too aggressive?

All of these thoughts were quickly put to rest when she saw his turn signal come on a little way ahead of her. Her heart sank as she read the sign in front of the building.

"Gettysburg Cancer Center."

She pulled into a parking space a few rows down from Evan and watched him walk into the building. She wanted to go in but was paralyzed with fear. A part of her felt like she had known this man for years and in her mind, was very comfortable being around him. She felt as if she could tell him anything. She sat in the car, deep in thought.

After what seemed like forever, Evan came out, got into his SUV and left.

She couldn't explain why or how, but she cared about this man so much already and she had to know what was wrong with him. He had no family, or anyone to take care of him. This deeply troubled her. After she was sure he was gone, Katie got out of her car and walked into the Cancer Center.

"May I help you?" asked the nurse behind the desk. Katie wasn't sure what to say.

"Um yes, the guy who was just in here, Evan Walker - is his doctor around, I'd like to speak to him please," said Katie.

"Are you a family member?" asked the nurse.

She was already on a roll with the lies so she had no problem adding another.

"Yes, I'm his sister," said Katie.

"One moment." The nurse dialed a number on the phone.

"Thank you," said Katie. She couldn't hear what the nurse was saying over the phone, but then she hung up.

"Doctor Spangler can see you for a few minutes. Go through those doors and his office is the third door on the right," said the nurse.

"Third door…thank you" Katie said once again.

Her heart pounded as she went through the doors and started down the hallway. She came to the door that read 'Dr. Spangler' and knocked.

"Come in," she heard a male voice call out. She nervously opened the door.

"Hello, what can I help you with," said the older, gray haired man sitting behind his desk.

"Thank you for seeing me Dr. Spangler, I'm here about Evan Walker."

"Who did you say you were? His sister? I wasn't aware Evan had any family," said the doctor. Katie looked at the ground, then back towards the doctor.

"I'm not his sister, and you're right, he has no family. I'm someone that cares deeply about him and I'm worried. He won't tell me anything. Can you please tell me what's going on with him?" said Katie, tears now streaming down her face.

"I'm sorry, but if you're not family I'm…." the doctor said but was quickly cut off.

"Please, he has nobody and if I can help him I want to do everything in my power to do that." Katie was sobbing now. The doctor stared at her for a moment and could see the pain she was going through.

"I'm sorry miss but patient records are confidential."

"Oh my God it's something bad isn't it," she sobbed.

"Miss, I'm sorry. I wish I…."

"Whatever it is, what if I told you I can help him with whatever needs to be done."

"Evan's been stubborn when it's come down to this," Dr. Spangler said.

"Come down to what? Please tell me doctor. I want to help him."

"Evan has pancreatic cancer," said the doctor. "He frustrates me. He won't get the needed surgery that will give him a chance. He comes in for chemo treatments to, as he says, get him by to write one more good book."

Katie was stunned. "What do you mean, give him a chance? How bad is he?" said Katie.

The doctor was silent for a minute.

"I give him a year to live," he finally said.

Katie, through sobbing eyes, stared at him in disbelief. "Does he know this?" she asked.

"Yes, of course he does but he says he can't afford it, he's lived a decent life and he feels it's his time so he isn't going to fight it," said the doctor.

Katie suddenly heard Evan's voice in her head saying five little words from the night before…."*It is what it is!*"

"Doctor Spangler, what if I paid for the surgery, would he have a chance then," said Katie, tears still streaming down her face.

"There's a ninety-eight percent chance of a full recovery with surgery. That is, if you get him to agree to it. He's a stubborn man," said the doctor.

"It's a very expensive surgery. Are you sure you can afford it?" added the doctor.

For the first time since her visit to Gettysburg, Katie was going to use her name to make a difference. She grabbed her wallet out of her purse and pulled out her driver's license and credit cards. It didn't take the doctor long to realize who she really was and she was not kidding about paying whatever it took.

"You make the arrangements as soon as possible and I will have him here," said Katie.

"You know Miss Chambers, I've been doing this for quite a long time. I try not to get close to patients because, to be brutally honest, sometimes things don't always turn out the way we want them to. Evan has frustrated me because I've always believed if he tried, he'd have a chance. I don't know how you two met, or why. But I do believe everything happens for a reason. Do what you have to do to convince him to come in and we'll be ready."

Katie shakes Dr. Spangler's hand, thanks him and returns to the car. She pulled out her phone and sent a text to Evan.

'Are you up for some dinner and showing me around some more places tonight' it read.

Beep, went her phone. 'Sure, is four ok?' was the response she got.

'Perfect, see you at the hotel' she replied. Now she had to think of a plan to confront Evan.

Katie drove the car back to the hotel, thanked Jennifer then walked the streets for a bit of window shopping before returning to her room to get her thoughts in order. As she stretched out on her bed, a million thoughts ran through her head. She kept trying to think of the perfect words to say, or how to even bring the matter up. But after a while her eyes grew weary and soon she fell fast asleep.

7

Katie was awakened by the sound of her ringing phone. She looked at her watch. It was five after seven already.

"Dammit," she said out loud. She scrambled to grab her things and rush out the door.

Once outside, bright sunlight hit her eyes which made her comically look like someone with a hangover. She frantically grabbed sunglasses from her purse and put them on. Katie looked in the window of Evan's SUV and saw him sitting in the driver's seat laughing hysterically. Embarrassed or not, seeing the laughing grin on his face instantly brought her ease and even made her laugh along with him as she opened the door.

"Well good morning sleeping beauty," he said as she climbed into the passenger's seat. Katie looked at Evan with a silent smile. Staring at his smiling face, she almost forgot how sick he was.

"I'm sorry, this town is too relaxing," she retorted. "I can't stop falling asleep!"

"Why do you think I moved here Dawn," Evan quickly said. "This town is a magical place where magical things can happen."

"What do you feel like eating tonight? Italian? Mexican? A sub? Pizza?"

"I really enjoyed the Italian place. Could we go there again?" answered Katie.

"Italian it is Dawn. But first I'd like to show you some cool places if you're not too hungry and would like to see them first."

For the first time since she started spending time with Evan, Katie felt guilt when she heard the name Dawn out loud and she almost confessed. But now wasn't the time.

"No, that sounds great. I'm not that hungry yet. Let's go."

Evan drives Katie to the Gettysburg Visitors Center and parks. As they walk towards the entrance chatting, Katie remembers the first time she was here with Tommy and how miserable she felt. Now, being here with Evan a smile shone brightly upon her face. They enter the building.

"This is where I first saw your book. What else is here," Katie asks.

"A painting."

"Must be a great painting to be hanging in a place like this."

"Oh, you're about to see for yourself," said a smiling Evan.

Evan buys two tickets for the Cyclorama. He hands Katie her ticket. She reads it.

"Cyclorama? I thought you were going to show me a painting."

"Be patient young lady, you'll see the painting soon enough."

The two are led into a small theatre where they watch a quick movie and are then told to proceed out the exit and up the escalator. Evan stands behind Katie to see her reaction as they slowly make their way to the top. Katie's jaw drops as they reach the top and she sees the giant painting that circles the entire room.

"Wow! Evan, I'm speechless."

"You like it?"

"It's amazing."

They listen to the guide tell the story of the painting then of the battle itself. Katie walks the room in awe, staring at the details of the painting, as does Evan, even though he's seen the painting many times. After the presentation is over, they walk down the stairs, exit the building, walking to the parking lot and get into Evan's SUV to leave.

"I never get tired of going there," said Evan.

"I hated history in high school but I'm really enjoying seeing some of the things here. I never knew."

Katie pulls Evan towards her, hugs him and starts to cry.

"Thank you Evan."

"For what?"

"For being nice to me. For making me laugh. Making me remember what it's like to be truly happy again."

"Um, you're crying. You sure everything is okay?"

"It will be. Soon, very soon."

"You hungry yet? Ready for some food," Evan asks.

"Sounds great. Let's eat."

The two drive across town and pull into the parking lot of the Italian restaurant where they have a fabulous dinner and conversation. Katie was in awe of Evan's strength and positivity to completely ignore what was going on in his private life and make this all about her. Nobody had ever treated her that way.

Being who she was and living in Hollywood, people usually tried to please Katie. Of course, they usually had hidden agendas and wanted to be around her to share the spotlight. Not Evan. This was genuine. Katie was just an everyday girl to him and he treated her like anyone else he'd ever showed around Gettysburg, which in some crazy way made her love him even more. *Love!* The word she heard in her head jolted her into reality. She had only known this man for a few days but it was then that she realized *she was in love with him.* The kind of love she had only read about in her movie scripts.

"I almost forgot to ask, how did your appointment go today?"

"Meh, just another appointment. The usual."

"Are you sure everything is okay? Wouldn't lie to me would you?"

"Everything is fine. Just a little problem with my thyroid. Levels are off a bit, whatever that means."

"Okay, just checking."

"Enough about me. How was your day before I picked you up? Do anything exciting? Tons of gift shops in this town.

Now was not the time for Katie to tell Evan she had followed him to the doctor's office and knew the truth.

"I walked the streets for a while. I saw one of those old-time photo shops and thought about getting one done dressed up in period attire."

"You should totally do that. You would look hot in one of those old dresses, well, not that you wouldn't look beautiful in anything really, but yeah, you should do that. I'll even pay for it."

"That sounds like a dare."

"Oh, it's a dare, trust me."

"You're on! But if I have to do it then you're doing it too. And you have to let me pay for yours."

"Ouch! Double dare!"

"That's the deal. I do it, you do it!"

"Well played. Well played!"

"It's settled then. Next time we're close to the photo shop we are getting it done."

The two finish dinner and get back in his SUV Evan asks Katie if there was anyplace she had in mind to see.

"I'd love to see the Triangular Field. From your experiences you wrote about in your book that sounds like a cool place."

"Triangular Field it is," said Evan as he steered his SUV out of town and towards the battlefield. They parked, got out of his truck and started walking towards an old, worn, rickety gate at the top of the field.

"See that gate?" asked Evan. "If you go past that gate with any kind of electronic equipment it usually fails," he added. He told Katie the story of a visit from his uncle and cousin. He was showing them around and they had come to this place. He told them the story of the gate, and his cousin, being a skeptic, didn't believe in the old legend. She had brought a brand-new camera with her that day and it worked great all morning and into the early afternoon. When she walked through the gate and into the field, her camera quit working. She looked at Evan, who by this time had a 'I told you so" look on his face with a sly smile. Her camera never worked again the rest of the trip. She later informed him that she took it back to where she bought it and they had no idea why it quit working, nor could they fix it. They did give her a new one but all the photos from that day were lost forever. After hearing his story, Katie couldn't wait to see what might happen when she crossed past the gate of the unknown. The only thing she had was her cellphone, so she turned it on, made sure it was fully charged and walked into the field to take some photos. She snapped only three photos before her phone suddenly went dead. Katie pressed the button to turn it back on, but got nothing.

"What the hell!" she said out loud, then looked back towards Evan, who by this time was smiling ear to ear.

"Don't ever doubt me young lady," he said with a laugh. Katie shook her head in disbelief and smiled back.

"I think you've seen enough of this place, let's get you out of here and hopefully your phone will start working when we leave" said Evan.

"It better or you're in deep trouble mister," she joked.

"Hey, I tried to warn you," Evan joked.

They both laughed as they walked from the field, back to his SUV and drove away. Driving through the battlefield Evan pulls off to the side of the road and pointed out a monument to Katie.

"See that? It's the Irish Brigade Memorial, one of my favorite monuments on the battlefield," said Evan.

"I want a picture of it," said Katie as she grabbed her phone, but forgot it had shut off. She hit the power button and her phone came back to life.

"Oh my God, the power is even full," she said in amazement.

"Again, welcome to Gettysburg," Evan said with a laugh. Katie climbed from the SUV and walked over to the monument to take some photos. She stood at the base, gazing upward at the huge Celtic Cross made of bronze. Katie noticed a dog lying at the foot of the cross.

"Evan, what kind of dog is this?"

"It's an Irish Wolfhound," he answered.

This is beautiful, she thought as she snapped a few photos then returned to the SUV.

By now it was getting dark and the time they could spend in the park was ticking down.

"What next?" asked Evan.

"Wouldn't it be cool if we had one of those cameras like they use in the TV shows, you know, the ones that show hot and cold temperatures," said Katie.

"You mean a FLIR?" asked Evan.

"Yes, one of those things," she said with a giggle.

"I do have one," said Evan with a smile.

"NO WAY!" Katie clapped her hand over her mouth when she realized how loud and excited she sounded.

"Well, I don't have it with me, but it's back at my place," said Evan.

"Can we go get it? Pleeaasseeeee," Katie said sounding like a teenage schoolgirl. Her voice made Evan laugh out loud.

"Sure, my place isn't too far from here," he said.

Katie was in her glory and could barely sit still as they drove back to Evan's apartment and parked his SUV.

"Can I come with you?" asked Katie.

"As long as you don't mind steps," Evan joked. She followed him through the front entrance and up the three flights of stairs it took to get to his apartment. When they got to his front door and he reached for his keys, Evan looked at Katie for a second.

"Just promise me one thing. It's not much - so don't laugh," he said.

"I promise," she said, realizing that her heart felt what was inside his.

Evan unlocked his door and they entered the now dark apartment lit only by three timer candles. He flipped on a few lights and when he did, Katie was for some reason floored. She was expecting a typical guy's messy man cave but instead she was seeing a clean, beautifully decorated apartment with antiques, pictures, paintings, and lots and lots of candles. Katie stood in the living room speechless.

"Dawn, I told you it wasn't much," Evan laughed nervously.

It was at that moment that she knew this man was different and he had much to live for. Katie knew now was the time to confront Evan about his illness and somehow try to help him change his mind.

Katie walked into the kitchen. Evan had bottles of wine stored in a small wine rack. Evan walked into the kitchen right behind her holding his FLIR camera.

"I see you like wine," she said.

"I do occasionally. I've got wine, beer, soda, water....I've got it all," he said with a laugh.

"Would you like something? What's mine is yours," he said to Katie.

"A glass of wine would really hit the spot right about now," she said.

"Red or white, my lady?" he said in the worst possible English butler accent ever.

Katie laughed.

"Red please," she said.

Evan opened a bottle of his favorite red wine, one made locally in Gettysburg. He poured them each a glass.

"Let's sit on the balcony," he said, opening the sliding glass door to the outside. Once again, Katie was speechless. Evan had it decorated with fake, but real looking leaves of foliage and little white lights all the way around the railing, topped off with a centennial flag that was blowing slightly in the wind. He also had real flowers growing in a pot with solar lights illuminating them.

He lit a candle that was sitting on the table and turned on a flickering electric candle encased in a lantern just above them. It was such a relaxing setting, Katie started to rethink her plan. Maybe this wasn't the time to confront Evan about his illness. But she knew the clock was ticking, and if she cared about this man at all. Now was the time to speak up.

"It's so beautiful out here," said Katie while looking up at all the bright, twinkling stars that lit up the night sky.

"I come out here and write quite a bit. Especially at night when it's quiet," said Evan.

"Are you working on anything right now?" asked Katie.

"I am in fact," said Evan. The words have been coming slow, so I hope to have it done within a year," he joked.

His words did not get the response he was hoping for. When Katie heard the words 'hope to have it done within a year', she broke down. She tried to hide it a first, but Evan noticed the tears now streaming down her face.

"Dawn, what's wrong?" His expression was one of panic. "Did I say something to upset you?"

Katie stared at Evan for what seemed like an eternity, trying to find the right words.

"Evan, I'm so, so sorry." She was sobbing now.

"I don't understand. What are you sorry for?" asked Evan.

"The other day, when I didn't really know you all that well, I followed you," said Katie.

"You followed me?" asked Evan. What do you mean you followed me?"

"To the doctor's office," she said shamefully.

"Oh that. It's okay. Don't be sorry. It is what it is." Evan smiled, trying to comfort Katie.

Katie's eyes widened. His words almost made her angry. "Why are you not trying to fight this? It's not fair! I finally meet this great guy only to find out his time here is limited," she said.

"I'll tell you what's not fair," said Evan calmly. "Little kids that get cancer, or some other horrible illness that they don't deserve. Little children that haven't had a chance to live, to experience life. Little kids that suffer at such a young age. To me, that isn't fair," he added.

His words made perfect sense, but still, she couldn't comprehend why he didn't want to fight this disease.

"I've lived a good life. I have a few regrets but I've honestly lived a good life. To be completely honest with you Dawn, it's the loneliness. It's already killed me. I have no family, very few people I can call close friends. Sure, I have friends, well, I'll just call them acquaintances. Do you know how depressing it is to spend holidays by yourself? To walk through town seeing families and couples enjoying time with each other, laughing, smiling, happy? Do you know what it feels like to have nobody to care for you? To love you? It's not the way you want to spend your life….trust me." He looked down at their glasses of wine, the twinkling sting of lights flickering, reflecting inside each circled top.

"When the doctor told me about this, it was in a weird, crazy way a relief. It's my ticket out of here. Besides Dawn, do you have any idea of the costs involved? Writers don't write to become rich. I'd be in debt for the rest of my life," he added. Evan started to speak again but was quickly cut off by Katie.

"Nobody cares for you? Are you serious? I know this will sound totally insane, but I fell in love with you the first day I met you. Hell, I fell in love with you just from skimming through your books and I hadn't even met you yet. So DON'T sit here and tell me nobody loves and cares about you, because I'm sitting right in front of you," she said.

Evan was stunned. He sat speechless, staring at Katie.

"Well?" Katie got up from her chair and walked to the other side of the table to where Evan was sitting. She gently placed both of her hands upon his cheeks.

"You're not alone. I'm here for you. Together we can beat this."

Hearing her words, Evan started to cry. He tried to speak but no words came out. Katie wrapped her arms around him. He wrapped his arms tightly around her, never wanting to let go. They looked at each other for a few seconds while Katie wiped his tears and then kissed him. The kiss was magical, and for the first time in many years they both felt as if they weren't alone anymore.

"Will you do me a favor and go to the doctor with me?" asked Katie.

"Dawn, I told you, I just don't have the money, I appreciate it but...."

Katie cut him off. "I have the money and will take care of everything," she said.

"You have that kind of money lying around? How?"

"Come here." She grabbed Evan's hand and led him back inside. Earlier, while standing in the living room, she noticed that he had a DVD case filled with movies. Katie started going through Evan's collection of movies.

"We going to watch a movie?" he asked in a comedic tone as if to lighten the mood.

Katie didn't answer as she continued looking through his collection of movies. Finally, she stopped, picked out a DVD and held it behind her back.

"I have something I need to tell you, and please don't be angry with me. I did what I did because it felt so good to just be a normal person again. To be treated like anyone else. You did that for me and I can't tell you how great that made me feel."

"What are you talking about?" He stared into her eyes as confusion filled Evan's own.

She unveiled the DVD she was hiding behind her back and held it up in front of Evan. The DVD was one of her movies, and her picture graced the cover. "Evan, my name isn't Dawn. I *am* Katie Chambers."

8

Evan stood quietly for a moment, trying to process the words he had just heard. He looked bewildered, but finally replied. "No way!"

"Evan, it is me, really," Katie said softly. "I was enjoying being a 'normal' person. I'm sorry I lied to you. Believe me, I've never been sorrier. If I had told you who I really was, would you have treated me differently?" she asked.

She had a great point and he knew it. "You're right, yeah. I probably would have. You would've intimidated the shit out of me," he said. "Why are you here in Gettysburg of all places? You could be anywhere in the world," he added.

Katie looked at Evan with a smile. "Let's just say fate brought me here. It wasn't planned by any means. I ended up here, stumbled upon your books, felt a need to find you and talk to you. I stumbled upon you that morning when we were both out taking the sunrise photos. I mean really Evan, for both of us to be in the same place at the same time. And I didn't have any idea of where I should go. I went with my instincts and there you were. You can't deny that was fate," she said.

"I've always believed in the whole fate, everything happens for a reason thing so you're not going to get any arguments from me," he joked. They both stood smiling at each other. "Well holy shit, Katie Chambers is standing in my living room," he said, with a sly smile on his face.

"I'm the same girl you spent the last few days with. Nothing has changed," she said as she reached up and put her arms around his shoulders. "I'm the same girl that for reasons unknown, fell in love with this great guy from Gettysburg, Pennsylvania that she even barely knows but wants to know everything about and spend every second of every day with," she said as she stared into his eyes."

"Yep, you're definitely right, now I'm intimidated. The famous actress Katie Chambers just said she was in love with me," he said with a smile.

"You're such a smartass," she said and the grip she had around his shoulders became even stronger. She held him tightly in her arms, then backed away for a second. "And Katie Chambers wants to help you get better so you can be around for her for many, many more years to come," she said with a serious look. "Will you please let me help you?" she asked.

"Seriously, that's too much money to be asking of anyone," said Evan.

"Just shut up, say yes, and come to the doctor with me," she said. "Besides, I need you to stick around. Someone has to write this story that's unfolding between us so I can send it to Hollywood and star in it when it becomes a movie," she said with a laugh.

"See, I knew there was a catch," he said laughing.

"Will you please come with me first thing in the morning," she said.

Evan let out a big sigh.

"Okay, you win," he said.

Katie leapt into his arms, crossed her legs around his and kissed him full on the lips.

Evan backed up towards the couch and gently laid down with Katie still in his arms. It felt great to be holding someone who cared about him once again. It seemed like forever ago since he'd felt like this. He looked at the clock on the wall which now read twenty minutes after ten.

"Well, the parks closed now. So much for taking the FLIR out. Do you have any ideas of what you want to do now?" he joked.

"Exactly this," she blushed and looked down.

When she looked at Evan, Katie knew he must feel the same emotions that flooded her body and mind. This moment - this very moment - is what Katie had been missing in her life. She planned to enjoy every second of it.

"Wait one minute, something's missing." Evan jumped up.

"Where are you going?"

Evan smiled as he moved from candle to electric candle. Flipping each one on. They were fake, but looked real when they were all lit. He slipped back onto the couch and took Katie in his arms.

"There, how's that?" he asked.

"Perfect, everything is perfect."

They laid on the couch talking and getting to know each other. The more they communicated, the more they fell in love.

The clock on the wall read three-thirty in the morning.

"Geez, look at the time. Where did it go?" he asked Katie.

She looked, but said nothing.

"Are you hungry?"

"Is anything open this late?" asked Katie.

"Do you really want to leave? How about I make you some breakfast," he suggested.

"You cook?" There was surprise in her voice.

"A little," laughed Evan. "How does French toast and eggs sound?

"Mmmmm sounds great," said Katie.

"Turn on the TV and make yourself comfortable then while I get this around," said Evan.

While channel surfing, Katie stopped when she came to a picture of herself on the screen. It was a popular tabloid show and below her photo were the words, 'Katie Chambers missing, whereabouts unknown.' It jolted her, but then she realized she had switched her cell phone to 'airplane mode' after meeting up with Evan earlier in the day. She only used it to take a photo of the monument, otherwise the phone was useless. She had planned to confront him and didn't want any distractions. She switched it back only to get another jolt. One hundred and thirty-eight missed calls. Two hundred and four text messages and fifty-two voice mails. All at once she realized Evan was quietly standing behind her with a smile.

"You're in big trouble missy," he said with a laugh.

The last thing she wanted to do was look at her phone, but she knew she had to let someone know she was okay. She scrolled through text messages from friends and family, only choosing to read the important ones. She then looked through her missed calls. Most were from her mother.

"I have to call my mom and let her know I'm okay," Katie said.

He poked his head around the corner. "Sure, I'll be right here in the kitchen."

Katie dialed her mother's phone.

Evan was in the kitchen but could hear a few words coming from Katie.

"Trust me, Mom, I'm okay. I'm the happiest I've been in years. Please don't worry. I'll call you later and explain all of this. I love you! Talk soon...."

Evan then he heard her phone beep off. "Everything okay?" he asked.

"As long as my mom knows I'm okay that's all that matters and now she knows, so yep, everything is perfect," she said.

Just then the words 'Breaking News' flashed upon the screen. 'Katie Chambers located.'

"Damn, that was quick," joked Evan.

"Gotta love the Hollywood gossip!" Katie laughed.

"I told mom to call my agent and let her know everything is fine and I'm just taking a little rest," she added.

"Well don't rest too long, your food is ready," he said with a smile.

Katie sat at the little pub table Evan had in his kitchen as he placed the plates of eggs and French toast in front of her.

"This looks SO good," she said.

"Thank you." Evan hopped into the chair across from her. They sat, ate and talked. A candle that Evan had turned on earlier was lit, flickering between them. As they sat at the table talking, Katie realized that this was the first time a guy had done something nice for her without no expectation of getting something in return. Even before she was famous, guys would ask her out, treat her to dinner and expect more than just a thank you kiss. When she was famous, people were even quicker to always have an ulterior motive. Perhaps money, a role in one of her movies, it always seemed to be something. But not Evan.

She knew he was different and with each gesture of kindness he offered, asking nothing in return, she beamed with joy. He hadn't even wanted her to help save his own life, and that spoke volumes.

"My gosh, it's almost five in the morning,"

Evan's words pulled Katie from her thoughts.

"I'd better get you to your hotel so you can get some sleep. I'm so sorry I kept you up all night," he added.

"Come here."

She led him by the hand to the couch. "Do you think we could just lie here like we did earlier and fall asleep together?" she asked.

Evan grabbed a blanket from his closet and jumped on the couch with his arms wide open.

Katie grinned and fell into his arms.

He gently placed the blanket over them both and they held each other tight, as they both closed their eyes and fell fast asleep

Evan awoke to bright daylight shining through the doors leading to his balcony. Katie was still asleep, her arms holding him tightly. *What a way to wake up, this feels so good,* he thought. He looked at the clock on the wall which now read eight forty-five. He'd have to wake Katie sooner or later but he hesitated. He wanted to stay in that moment forever.

"Katie, Katie, it's time to get up," Evan whispered in her ear.

Katie let out a cute little moan, stretched, and then held Evan closer. "What time is it?' she mumbled.

"Almost nine. You want some coffee?" he asked.

"Absolutely!"

Evan rose from the couch and into the kitchen. While he poured each of them a cup of coffee he heard Katie groan so he knew she was up and stretching.

"Cream and sugar right?"

"You remembered, I'm impressed." Katie walked into the kitchen, put her arms around Evan's waist and kissed him.

"Well good morning to you too" he said with a smile. "You drink your coffee while I hop into the shower. I'll be right back."

While he headed off towards the bathroom. Katie took her coffee and sat out on the balcony to wait. It was a cool morning. The birds were chirping and other than the traffic noise coming from Route Thirty it was quiet and peaceful outside. She sat in deep thought, thinking about the doctor visit that was quickly approaching. She was glad Evan decided to do what was needed but it still made her nervous. Katie knew a lot of people but never knew of any of them to have an illness of this kind. These overwhelming feelings were new to her.

"There you are," she heard a voice say.

Evan stood in the doorway wearing only jeans.

Very nice! she thought, reveling in the sight standing in front of her.

"I'm almost ready, but would you like another cup of coffee?" he asked.

Katie looked at her cup. She was so deep in thought that she had barely touched her coffee. "No, I'm good thank you," she said.

"Okay, be right back."

After watching him disappear once again, Katie walked back inside to look around Evan's apartment. She hadn't had a chance to see anything except the living room and kitchen the day before. She walked into his home office. The walls were decorated with a few of his favorite movie posters, some civil war memorabilia and photos of Evan with people she didn't recognize but the pictures were autographed so they must have been someone that meant something to him. She looked at his glass desk and saw a stack of business cards among other items that sat perfectly in place, including an autographed baseball.

"Evan, can I steal one of your business cards?" she called.

"Sure, but be sure to blow the dust off first," he joked.

She grabbed a couple from their holder and held them in her hand as she entered his bedroom. The furniture was beautiful, especially his bed, complete with a European down comforter and big frilly pillows.

This man is truly special, she thought. *What guy makes his bed?* The walls didn't have much on them, but she did notice what looked like an old barn window filled in with quilted patterns hanging above his bed. She left the bedroom and stopped at the bathroom door where Evan was brushing his teeth.

"Almost done," he said.

"You know, for a guy, you have very good taste," she said with a smile.

"Thank you, it's not much but I try to make it cozy in here."

"I changed my mind, is it okay if I make myself another cup of coffee?"

"What's mine is yours, help yourself."

Katie walked into the kitchen to make herself a fresh cup. Another thing she had never noticed before were the wine bottles adorned with decorative ivy that Evan had placed around the top of his cupboards. She finished making her coffee and opened the freezer to throw an ice cube in it. Evan was almost ready to go. This would cool it off so she could drink it quickly.

"Ready when you are." said Evan strolling into the kitchen.

Katie sipped her coffee. "Almost done. Oh, do you have Dr. Spangler's phone number I'd like to call him," she said.

Evan scrolled through the contacts in his phone until he got to the doctor. He hit the 'dial' button and handed the phone to Katie.

"Hello, could I speak to Dr. Spangler please?" she said. "Thank you," she added.

A minute went by and as she waited Katie finished her coffee.

"Yes, hello, Dr. Spangler, this is Katie Chambers, we spoke about Evan yesterday and he's agreed to do the procedure. Could we see you this morning?"

Evan watched as Katie listened to the doctor speak.

"Great, thank you, we'll see you then," she said, hanging up the phone and turning to Evan. "Okay we have two hours," she said.

"Then we better get you to your hotel so you can shower and change." Evan grabbed his keys and cell phone.

Together, they left his apartment, walked down the steps, got into his SUV, and drove towards her hotel. Once there, he parked and they went into Katie's room where she grabbed her bag, told Evan to watch TV and she'd be right out.

Evan heard the shower water come on. He sat in the chair flipping through the TV stations. Nothing good was on so he turned it off. He noticed his books lying all over

Katie's bed. He picked up the book of photos and skimmed through it. This book was now very special to him. After all, it was the book that - for reasons unknown to him – had drawn her to him. He heard her blow dryer start up so he knew she was close to being done. Within a few minutes, she emerged from the bathroom dressed and ready to go.

"You ready?" she asked.

"Not really but I guess I promised you so let's get this over with," he joked as they left her hotel room. Before they got into his SUV, Katie turned to Evan.

"Could I ask you something?"

"Sure, what is it?"

"Would it be bold of me to ask if I could stay with you instead of here at the hotel?"

Evan answered without missing a beat. "I'd be honored," he said.

All at once, Katie spun around. "I'll be right back," she said as she shot back into the hotel. She reappeared with her suitcase, threw it in the back of his SUV then climbed into the passenger seat.

They arrived at the parking lot of the Gettysburg Cancer Center, parked and walked into the doctor's office.

"Good morning Evan, Dr. Spangler will be with you in a minute," said the receptionist.

"Thank you." He and Katie sat down in the waiting area. They had barely gotten comfortable when the door opened and Dr. Spangler called Evan back to his office. Katie followed. Once inside he closed the door behind them.

"Thank you both for coming in, and Katie, thank you for getting him here," said the doctor.

"Thank you for seeing us so quickly, I really appreciate it," she said.

"Do either of you have any questions for me?" asked Dr. Spangler.

Katie responded quickly. "How soon can we get Evan in?"

"Actually young lady, I've been waiting for this moment for months, hoping he would change his mind. I cancelled the rest of my office appointments for the day and have him scheduled for surgery in about an hour."

"An hour," said a surprised Evan. "I wasn't prepared for it being this soon," he added.

"Had you agreed to do this when we first diagnosed it, everything would have been over by now. But the truth of the matter is that we need to get this done immediately. And I'm going to be upfront with you. Waiting this long, there are risks involved but we won't know how bad it is until we see exactly what we're dealing with - once we get you in the operating room."

Evan looked at Katie. She could see the fear in his eyes. He had been brave and seemingly uncaring up until this point. But she knew that hearing the doctor's words had forced reality to set in and he *was* scared.

She put a hand on his knee. "Hey, you're not alone anymore. I'm right here by your side and I'm not going anywhere, ever! We're in this together."

Evan smiled at Katie, then turned. "Okay doc, let's do this."

Dr. Spangler led Evan and Katie out of his office, down a hallway and to an elevator. Once inside, the doctor pressed the button to the fourth floor where they got off.

"Evan, you come with me and Miss Chambers, please wait in the waiting room to your right. I'll be in to get you when we're all finished," said Dr. Spangler.

Katie wrapped her arms around Evan for a hug and a kiss before letting him go.

"I'll be waiting for you right here," she said as he and the doctor walked down the hallway and disappeared behind a door.

The waiting room was empty. She grabbed a magazine and sat down in a chair. She looked at the clock hanging on the wall. It was one thirty-five in the afternoon. As she flipped through the pages of the magazine her eyes started to close. Even without much sleep the night before she had to be strong for Evan. Katie put down the magazine and made herself a cup of coffee. While gazing out the windows that overlooked Gettysburg she imagined living there the rest of her life with Evan. That's when it hit her. She would give up everything for this guy. Hollywood was full of fake people and this, to her, was real. And she liked this kind of life much better.

After finishing her coffee and reality daydream, she went back to her seat and picked up another magazine. Then, she heard a door open.

Dr. Spangler walked into the waiting room. The look on his face was not at all what Katie hoped to see. She knew something was wrong.

"How is he doctor? Is everything okay?"

"I'm sorry Katie, we did everything we could. There was just too much damage already done. He didn't make it, I'm so sorry."

"What? No! You said he had a chance! No! No! No!" Katie sobbed.

Dr. Spangler put his hand on her shoulder.

"You can go back and see him if you'd like."

"No, this is not happening! Evan!"

Dr. Spangler again put his hand on her shoulder. She brushed it off.

"Are you okay dear?" Dear, are you okay?

Katie heard a woman's voice talking to her. She had fallen asleep. It was only a dream.

She looked up from her chair to see the same old woman she saw smiling at her on her first day in Gettysburg.

"Hello Katie, you must have been having a bad dream dear," she said.

She must recognize me from my movies, Katie thought.

"Hello, thank goodness yes, it was only a dream." she said to the woman.

"How is Evan doing? Have you heard anything?"

"Oh, you know Evan?" asked Katie.

"You could say that, but I haven't seen him for a while." She quietly laughed. "I heard he was here and just wanted to check up on him while I was in the area," she added.

"I was just about to make myself another cup of coffee, would you like a cup as well?" asked Katie.

As she turned to pour herself a cup of coffee she couldn't help but notice a beautiful Irish green emerald ring on the woman's finger. "That's a beautiful ring," Katie said.

"Oh, thank you dear, it was a gift from my husband. Speaking of him, I'd better get back. I told him I wouldn't be long. Just wanted to look in on Evan."

"Are you sure you wouldn't like a cup?" Katie turned, but the woman was gone. She walked to the hallway to look for her but she was nowhere to be seen.

"That was strange, she must have been in a hurry," she mumbled to herself, and then thought nothing more of it.

As Katie sipped her coffee Dr. Spangler walked into the waiting room with a smile. She sprang to her feet.

"How is he doing doctor?"

"He's a fighter. He's doing great, and surprisingly he's already awake if you'd like to go back and see him now."

"Yes, thank you."

"Dr. Spangler led Katie back through the winding hallways and into Evan's room.

As soon as Evan saw Katie a grin appeared on his face.

"I'll leave you two alone," said the doctor as he exited the room.

"Hey, how are you?" she whispered.

"A little sore, but better now that you're here. How are you doing?" he asked.

"Now that I know you're okay, I'm doing great," she said, kissing his cheek.

"Oh….there was someone here to see you a little while ago, an older lady. I actually ran into her twice before. Funny she knows you. I didn't even get her name she disappeared so fast. She wanted to check up on you but had to get back to her husband."

"That's strange," said Evan. "I wonder who that could be?"

"Yeah, tell me about it, the only thing I could tell you about her is that she wore this big, beautiful green emerald ring," Katie said.

Evan's eyes widened and Katie watched the emotions pass over his face. Puzzlement and then surprise. "What is it?" she asked.

"Did you say green emerald ring? Was it on her right hand?"

"Now that you say that, yes it was. Why, do you know her?"

"Could you bring me my wallet?" he asked.

Katie grabbed Evan's wallet and handed it to him. He opened it up, took out a photo and handed it to Katie.

"Was this the woman?" he asked.

"Yes! That's her. So you do know her. Why do you have her photo in your wallet? Is she a relative of yours?"

"Katie, this photo is of my mother."

Katie looked confused. "You told me you didn't have any family."

Evan gave Katie another chilling look, "I don't….my mother died over twenty years ago."

9

Over the next few days Evan's time at the hospital went quite well, and before they knew it Dr. Spangler had given him permission to spend the rest of his recovery at home, provided he agreed to have a home health aide drop by daily and someone would be with him around the clock.

"I'm not going anywhere, Doc," said Katie.

Evan is sent home and, as promised, Katie tends to his needs and helps the nurse when she drops by. After only a few days, Evan starts to feel guilty.

"Are you comfortable? Is there anything I can get you," Katie asks.

"Katie, you don't have to do all of this."

"I know I don't have to. I want to."

"Are you sure? I feel bad you're cooped up in this apartment all the time."

"And who am I cooped up with?"

"Me. That's why I'm sorry. I feel helpless why you do all the work."

"Hey, what did I tell you right before your surgery?"

"Hmmm, last thing I remember is you kind of yelled at me."

"There you go with the jokes again. That's right, I did. But I also said we were in this together. Me and you."

"Well I…."

"I wasn't done. Let me ask you something. Do you love me?"

"You have to ask? You are the best thing that has ever happened to me. And it's not because of who you are either. I mean, the celebrity thing. You could have told me you lived under a bridge and didn't have a dime to your name. I felt a connection to you that very first morning we met but I figured my time was limited so why even try for a relationship. I fell in love with who you are on the inside. Your heart. It's the kind of stuff I write about but never experienced until now."

Katie hugs Evan as tightly as she can without hurting him.

"Okay, now let me ask you this. If the tables were turned, would you mind taking care of me?"

"I would actually. This looks exhausting watching you do everything."

"You BETTER be joking mister," Katie laughed.

"Of course I am. I would take care of you no matter what. I'd be by your side day and night."

"Then you get it. So stop asking stupid questions, okay?"

"Did I miss something? Did we get married while I was out knocked out cold on the operating table?"

"I swear, every word that comes out of your mouth makes me laugh and love you even more."

"Oh, I'm sorry to hear that."

"See, stop it," she laughs.

"What if I did marry you while you were on that operating table. Would that be such a bad thing?"

"Not at all," Evan said with a serious look.

Katie holds him tightly in her arms.

"I think I'm ready to call it a night. Can I sleep with you in the bed instead of this couch," Evan asks.

"Are you sure you'll be comfortable in the bed? I'm afraid I might bump up against you and hurt you."

"I'll be fine. I want this. I need this. I want to hold you in my arms until we both fall asleep."

"I can't turn down a proposal like that now can I? Let me help you into bed."

Katie helps Evan into bed, makes sure he's comfortable, turns out the light and carefully cuddles next to him. They both smile as they hold each other.

"This is the best feeling in the world. I love you Katie."

Katie starts to cry.

"I never thought…."

"Hey, hey, hey what's wrong, are you okay?"

"I never thought I could be this happy. Thank you Evan, for everything."

"Thank you for trying to find me."

"I think we can both thank fate for that."

"Agreed."

"Good night Evan, I love you."

"Good night Katie, I love you. Sweet dreams."

Three weeks came and went quickly, and by then, Evan, with the help of his nurse and Katie was to the point where he was well enough to take short car rides and long walks around the battlefields. He almost felt back to normal with his camera around his neck, Katie by his side, and all the while taking in beautiful sunsets together. Those that didn't know him, would have never guessed he had been through such an operation.

On one particular evening Katie asked Evan if he'd like to go to Little Round Top to take photos and watch the sunset.

"That all depends….are you going to take some pictures too?" he asked.

"You know that all I have is my phone silly. I can't take very good pictures with that now can I?"

"Can you go into the closet in my office and grab the box that's right in front?" Evan asked.

When she had returned with the box she asked, "This one?"

"Open it," he said.

Katie gave him a curious look and lifted the lid to look inside. She gave him another confused look and asked, "What's this?"

"It's your new camera. I've been saving it in case my other one breaks, but I'd like you to have it."

Katie was speechless. Being a celebrity, she had received many gifts in her lifetime. But this one, this one touched her in a way she'd never been touched before. This was a gift from the heart. Evan's heart.

"Oh my God, I don't know what to say. Thank you SO much!" Katie wrapped her arms around him, pulling him close, in a huge hug.

"Ready to go try it out?" he asked.

Still smiling, she ran to the kitchen and grabbed the car keys.

"I'm ready when you are!"

Katie drove them to Little Round Top, parked the SUV, helped Evan grab their camera equipment and walked towards the summit. She wasn't surprised by how beautiful the sky looked. Every sunset seemed to be different here, always unique in its own way, as if God had a goal to appease the tourists who flocked to the national park.

Standing on the walkway, Evan stared at his favorite rock. Katie knew he was frustrated that he wasn't yet allowed to climb the rocks.

She looked around for a private location where there weren't many people around. "There, let's go sit over there," she said.

Evan followed her over to a secluded spot. When they got there, he showed her the settings on her new camera. He already had charged batteries packed, so her camera was ready to take pictures. Before long, Katie was snapping photos like a pro.

Evan watched the joy and excitement on her face. He was so happy for her that he never bothered to get his camera out of the bag. He simply sat quietly and enjoyed the moment.

Soon the sun had set and darkness had fallen.

"Are you hungry?" asked Evan.

"I am," she replied.

"What are you in the mood for tonight? Italian? Mexican? Chinese?"

"Actually, let's just grab a pizza on the way home, stay in and watch a movie. How does that sound to you?" Katie asked.

"Sounds perfect!"

They walked alone, down the path that led to the parking lot to where Evan's SUV was parked. Once inside Evan picked up his phone to call the local pizza shop. He put the phone back down and looked at Katie.

"I've got a better idea," he said.

"Yea?" she asked quizzically.

"How about some wine, ice cream and maybe a surprise?"

"Wine and ice cream at the same time? Katie said with a laugh.

"Just drive, I'll tell you where to go."

Katie pointed the SUV towards town and followed Evan's directions to an open parking spot on the street. They got out of the truck and walked to the winery where they bought a bottle of wine and found a table out back where live music played.

"And it took you this long to tell me about this place why?" asked Katie with a smirk.

"I forget about it sometimes, but after this you'll also enjoy the ice cream next door. It's the best in town."

"I may live in L.A. but this town seems to have everything you need and then some. I can see why it's so popular with tourists."

"Sometimes I take its small-town charm for granted. I never used to go out much, especially if I was alone. Kind of depressing seeing happy couples holding hands so I spend most of my time at home writing."

"You are not alone now so anytime you want to come back here or anywhere for that matter, I'll be right beside you."

"You're good at leaving me speechless sometimes, you know that?"

"Why would you say that?"

"Uh, because you are Katie chambers and I'm just some schmuck nobody from small-town U.S.A. I seriously still cannot fathom the fact that you are sitting here with me willingly and for some reason, in which totally baffles the living shit outta me, is you tell me you love me. It all just seems like a dream that's too good to be true."

Katie looks at Evan and smiles.

"You are right about one thing, I am Katie Chambers. But that doesn't matter. It's what I love about all of this. First of all, you are not a nobody. Have you read your own books? They are beautiful stories. If not for fate bringing me here I never would have saw them, read them and found the need to look for you. Everything happens for a reason Evan. I was miserable in California. Fed up with fake friends, fake people. It's real here. You're real. This is where I was meant to be and if you're a small-town schmuck then I'm happy to be a small-town schmuck too."

"Let me ask you one more question and if you answer it without hesitation I'll quit wondering."

"Fire away!"

"Are you seriously willing to give up everything you have just to be here with me?"

"I've already forgotten about it. I'm here now; this is where I belong. I know it in my heart."

"No hesitation whatsoever! I guess she means it folks!" Evan says comically.

"Oh yes she does," Katie said as she gets up and sits on Evan's lap. They kiss as relaxing live music plays from the small stage and a candle on the table romantically flickers in the breeze.

The two sit and talk under the dark, star-filled night sky. By looking at them, one would have thought they had been together for years.

They finished their wine and walked next door to Evan's favorite ice cream shop, a place called Mr. G's.

"Some old timers call this place the Twin Sycamores," Evan said, pointing to a single sycamore tree. "They once had two sycamores here to greet guests as they passed by. The one that is gone has been saved and used in very resourceful ways. When we get inside you'll see. One of the tables is actually made from the old tree."

"That is so cool! I love the way they try to keep everything historical."

"We definitely have history around here. No shortage in that department."

Evan knew Mike, the owner well and wanted Katie to meet him, but when they got inside he found out Mike wasn't there at the moment.

"I'll introduce you another time. He's a great guy and you will like him," Evan said as they walked to the dining area. She followed, to sit at the old wooden bar to enjoy their cones.

"Oh my gosh this ice cream is SO good. And this building; it's amazing!"

"I told ya you'd like it. See that table right there? That's made from the old tree I was telling you about."

"That is incredible."

Just then, Mike walked through the front door and saw Evan. As always, he greeted him with a handshake and a hug.

"Great to see you Evan," said Mike.

"Great to see you too Mike. I'd like you to meet Katie, and Katie this is Mike, the owner."

"I know who you are young lady. It's an honor to have you here. How's the ice cream?" Mike chuckled.

"Evan wasn't lying when he said you make the best ice cream. Now I know why he loves it here," she said.

"Well thank you, I appreciate that. Evan how are you feeling? I heard you had surgery or something?"

"Thanks to her I'm doing great. Enjoying life now so to speak."

"That's great to hear, I'm so glad. Katie, is Evan taking good care of you? Showing you everything our little town has to offer?"

"He certainly is. Just when I think I've seen the coolest thing he blows my mind with something else."

"That's what I like to hear. I hate to run but I have a million things do to. Very nice to meet you Katie, and Evan I'll see you soon."

Mike left the dining area, disappeared through a doorway and up a flight of stairs.

Evan and Katie finish their cones, walk outside and across the street where they stand on the sidewalk.

"Are you looking for someone," Katie asks.

"No why?"

"Are we standing here for a reason?"

"I promised you a surprise, didn't I?"

"How can you possibly top the wine and ice cream?"

"Not sure if I can top that but you'll see in a minute."

A beautiful, romantic, white horse drawn carriage pulls up in front of them and stops.

"Is this for us," Katie asks.

"After you my lady."

"Oh my God you are something else," Katie laughed.

Evan and Katie hold each other as the horse drawn carriage slowly makes its way around the streets of Gettysburg. The dark night lit by burning candles on each side of the carriage.

"Are you having a good time tonight?"

"Yes."

"You okay?"

"Uh-huh. I'm perfect. This is perfect. You are perfect. You're amazing Evan. This town is amazing. This sounds silly but, it's like I'm in a movie, only this is real and not a bunch of props. I keep waiting for the director to yell cut."

"You don't ever have to worry about anyone yelling cut again. Not on my watch anyway."

"Hold me tighter."

Evan holds her tight in his arms until the horse and carriage returns to the spot where it first picked them up. They get out and start walking through town.

"Evan, isn't your truck the other way?"

"Very observant, yes it is."

"Where are we going now? What are you up to?"

"Just want to check on something real quick, stay with me."

"Right beside you!"

Evan holds Katie's hand as they weave in and out of heavy night-time crowds that are also walking the streets of Gettysburg. They come to a corner where a woman dressed in a period attire dress and hat is running her ghost tour business. The woman and Evan make eye contact at the same time and give each other a hug.

"Cindy, it's great to see you. How are things going tonight?"

"Good to see you Evan. Things are busy as usual. Big crowds tonight so I'm not complaining."

"Cindy, I'd like you to meet Katie. Katie, this is Cindy, she's the owner and runs Sleepy Hollow Ghost Tours."

"I heard a rumor you were somewhere in town, it's very nice to meet you Katie."

"Very nice to meet you Cindy."

"I have to ask, how in the world did you get hooked up with this guy," Cindy asked teasingly.

"If I could explain it I'd be glad to tell you. I'll just say life has a funny way of working out, doesn't it?"

"Honey, I so agree."

"Any room left on one of your tours? I was hoping Katie could hear some of the local ghost stories," Evan asks.

"See that group over there in the parking lot? They just started. Come with me."

Cindy leads them over to the group. She informs the tour guide they will be joining the tour, then walks back to Evan and Katie.

"This is awesome. What do I owe you?"

"You know your money is no good here."

"Cindy, no, take this twenty, please."

She walks away without taking his money.

"Have a good time you two."

"She always does that. I'll sneak in and pay when we get back," Evan said.

"You have some amazing friends around here. They're real. True friends. That's hard to come by these days."

"They certainly are. I couldn't ask for better friends, that's for sure."

Evan and Katie blend in with the others already in the group as they walk the streets of Gettysburg listening to the tour guide tell stories of the ghosts that still roam the area. Soon they return to the parking lot where they had begun. Evan looks for Cindy but she's already left. He walks inside to pay for the tour then returns to Katie. He pulls out his phone and orders a pizza. He takes Katie's hand as they walk the now deserted, late night streets back to his SUV.

"You have fun tonight," he asks.

"I haven't had this much fun in I don't know how long. Thank you for everything Evan."

"You're very welcome, but tonight isn't over with yet. You still haven't tried the best pizza in Gettysburg."

"And a movie too. What are we watching," she asks.

"I'm not sure. I'll let you decide when we get back to my place."

"The perfect ending to a perfect evening," Katie said with a smile.

They arrive at his truck, go to pick up the pizza, then drive through the darkness of the battlefield to his apartment. Once parked, Katie grabbed the camera bags and Evan grabbed the pizzas. They made their way up the three flights of stairs and into his apartment.

Katie puts the camera bags away while Evan gets the plates, drinks and pizza ready.

"What movie would you like to…?"

Knock, knock, knock!

Evan was cut off by knocking on his front door. He and Katie looked at each other.

He walked to the door and opened it.

Standing in the doorway was Tommy Blake and a stern looking man in a dark, black suit.

Tommy turned and his eyes met Katie's.

"Well, well, well, look who it is!" Tommy said in a smug tone.

Anger flashed across Katie's face. "How did you find me?"

Tommy held up one of Evan's books, shaking it in the air.

"Wasn't hard. Small town. All I had to do was ask where he lived. I figured you'd be here," he added in the same smug tone. Tommy looked at Evan who was now standing by Katie's side. "Oh, where are my manners? How you doin' champ?" he asked Evan.

"What do you want?" Evan asked, trying to keep calm.

"We came for her, champ."

"I'm not going anywhere with you," Katie spoke up.

"Oh really? What do you think about that Mr. Nevins?" Tommy asked the man in the suit standing behind him.

"Miss Chambers, my name is Richard Nevins. I'm an attorney for RockWall Studios. I am here to inform you that you are now in breach of contract. Your failure to return with us will result in the studio having no choice but to file charges against you."

"File charges? That's bullshit!" said Katie.

"Miss Chambers, have you forgotten the studio has already paid you a substantial amount of money for your services. You signed a contract, and you were supposed to start shooting that movie last week. Our calls went unreturned and they had to get a replacement. They are, and I say this lightly, VERY upset with you! And may I further add, that your failure to return with us may lead to felony charges, restitution payment, and possibly jail time." Nevins said.

Katie's eyes started to water. Then tears.

"That's crap, you're just trying to scare her," Evan said.

"Stay out of this champ," smirked Tommy.

"Call me champ one more time, asshole, and I'll drop you," said Evan with a threatening look.

"Hear that Nevins, shall we add threat charges to all of this?" asked Tommy.

"I clearly heard a threat," said Nevins.

"This is all bullshit!" said a now agitated Evan.

"What's it going to be Katie? Your boyfriend is in this now. Hell, you'll both be in jail," Tommy said with a laugh. "Balls in your court!" he added.

Katie, now sobbing, turned to Evan. Tears rolled down her face. Evan held her tightly in his arms.

"Aw, isn't that sweet," smirked Tommy.

Evan glared at Tommy but said nothing.

Katie looked into Evan's eyes.

"I'm so sorry I got you into all of this. You made me forget about my old life and all of the problems and drama that went with it. You made me feel special. You made me feel normal. And most of all you made me feel truly loved and for that I can never thank you enough. Please don't be angry with me, but they're right," she said. I honestly never planned to leave you or this amazing town but I signed that contract and now I have to go face the consequences," said Katie.

"I'm not angry and I completely understand. You have to do what you have to do." Evan still held her tightly.

"Let's go, Katie. The car is waiting," said Tommy.

With that she let go of Evan, went into the bedroom to grab her bag and returned to the living room where she gave Evan one last hug before stumbling down the steps to climb into the car and leave with Tommy and Nevins.

Evan watched Katie walk down the stairs and disappear from sight. He shut the door and walked to his office window just in time to see the black limousine pull out of the apartment complex and onto Route Thirty. He walked from his office, through the living and into the kitchen where he saw the two pizza boxes sitting on the counter. He tried to be strong – he really did - but a tear ran down his face, and then another and another. He couldn't bear to look at the pizza boxes. Only moments ago, he and Katie had a wonderful, relaxing night planned.

He grabbed the pizza boxes, walked down the stairs and to the garbage dumpster sitting outside. He opened the lid, threw the boxes inside and stomped back up the stairs into his apartment. Standing in his kitchen, saddened beyond belief, a little sign he had hanging up caught his eye. It read, "It Is What It Is."

10

Evan stood there for a moment staring at the sign. He had hung that sign in that spot a long time ago, and for a very good reason. When things got tough, or were beyond his control, he always said these very words. And now, things were beyond his control and there was nothing he could do about it.

Perfect! He thought sarcastically.

He grabbed a beer from the refrigerator, opened it up and walked outside to the balcony where he sat quietly staring at the stars. He thought about his life and how it had changed in such a short period of time. A month ago he was dying, until this incredible generous girl appeared out of the blue and saved him.

The words she had spoken just a few moments ago still echoed in his mind. How could she even begin to think he would be mad at her for all she had done?

Done with his beer, he decided to try and sleep. It would get his mind off thinking about Katie.

After hours of tossing and turning he arose from his bed and got his laptop out, hoping to write something to take his mind off things, but that didn't work either.

He turned on the television, flipping through channels. His heart sank as he came upon a live news report. He watched as Katie walked through the Los Angeles Airport, cameras in her face as well as people asking questions as to her whereabouts. She looked very sad and kept her head down, talking to no one. He also noticed Tommy and Nevins walking behind her, both looking happy and smug at the same time.

Evan couldn't believe that just a few short hours ago, she was here with him and now she was all the way across the country.

He turned off the television, stretched out on the couch and forced himself to go to sleep. It wasn't long before the sound of a car door slamming woke him up. When he looked outside he realized it was only a nurse reporting to work at the nursing home next door. The clock read five twenty a.m.

He made himself a cup of coffee and decided to go for a drive and maybe take some sunrise photos. He grabbed his camera bag and proceeded down the stairs, opening the front door. He was shocked at the sight now before him.

Cameras flashed as a mad group of "paparazzi" ran towards him.

"Evan! Evan, can you tell us about your relationship with Katie Chambers," he heard one man scream out.

Where in the hell did all these people come from and how did they find out so damn fast? Like Katie had done, he lowered his head, talked to no one and got into his SUV.

Evan sped out of the parking lot before the mob could get into their cars and follow him. He knew all the backroads and shortcuts in and around town, so losing them was an easy task. He pulled his truck behind some trees and watched as the cars drove past one by one. He shook his head in disbelief.

If this is the way Katie has to live every day, no wonder she wasn't happy, was all Evan could think. He pulled his SUV from behind the cover of trees and drove in the opposite direction of the cars that had just passed.

Evan drove through the small alleyways around Gettysburg and parked behind the diner. He figured it was going to be a long day of cat and mouse so he'd better grab a bite to eat before going out to the battlefield to take some photos.

To his surprise, had an uneventful, quiet breakfast. He ate, paid, and then headed for his truck, which again, to his surprise was sitting alone with nobody waiting for him.

At the same time, out in California, Katie is on the set of her new movie. Filming isn't going well. The director and her co-stars are frustrated. This isn't the old Katie. She often finds herself daydreaming and forgetting her lines. Because of this, filming is taking longer than expected. After many tries at the same scene the director yells CUT, throws the script up in the air and drops his head in disgust. Tommy storms off the set in a huff. Katie stands alone, tears welling in her eyes.

Evan drives around the battlefields for hours. Not taking any photos, he spends the time thinking about what had happened. He went over it again and again. He thought about the last time he was out here was with Katie, and the hurt came again – wave after wave of agonizing pain. He was alone again, all alone.

He understood she had to leave, and that's just the way it had to be. She had her commitments that she had agreed to. But she was so far away, all the way across the country in California, and here he was, all alone in Pennsylvania.

Evan looked at his watch. It read one forty-five p.m.

These people aren't going to keep me from living my life, thought Evan as he drove back to his apartment. He looked around as he slowly drove his truck through the parking lot and was thrilled to see that nobody was there.

He parked the SUV, walked up the stairs and into his apartment, locking the door behind him.

Evan fixed himself some dinner and turned on the TV. While flipping through the channels he thought he saw himself. He proceeded to go back to the channel and sure enough, there he was on some useless tabloid show. *Unbelievable*, he thought.

Apparently, the paparazzi got what they had wanted, pictures of Evan.

Back in California, Katie's mother holds her as she's crying. Her mother knows the joy Evan brought to her daughter and that joy was taken away by greed. Her mother looks as heartbroken as Katie does.

Soon his phone beeped. It was a text from a number he did not recognize. It read: 'This is a friend of Katie. She wanted you to know she is deeply sorry for anything she has put you through.'

'Tell her I understand and I hope she is doing well. Thank you.' Evan sent the text back, and heard nothing more.

He changed the channel to a baseball game, ate his dinner and went to bed.

Over the next four months, life returned to normal for Evan. But normal without Katie was a different sort of normal. It still pained him whenever he drove past a location with memories of Katie, but he was moving on. She'd shown him that life was worth living. Writing once again, taking photos whenever he felt like it, he had a normal, boring life. He also couldn't help reading and hearing about the soon to be blockbuster movie Katie was working on. He saw her on talk shows, promoting the film, which some said would be her biggest movie to date.

Fall came to Gettysburg. The colorful leaves were at their peak and Evan went out every day to photograph breathtaking autumn scenes. He loved being outdoors this time of year.

One late afternoon, while driving by the local movie theatre Evan noticed a billboard promoting Katie's new movie. He read that tonight was its opening night all around the world. He thought about what they were most likely putting her through on this day. Getting fitted for the best, most expensive designer dresses to wear on the red carpet. He could only imagine the misery she was going through right now.

For a second he thought about turning around, driving to the theatre to watch it. But his heart wasn't in it. Maybe he'd buy the DVD when it came out, but he wasn't yet ready to sit and watch her for two hours. He couldn't admit it, but watching the movie would bring back too much pain, too much of what he missed.

He continued the drive up to Little Round Top so he could sit on his favorite rock and watch the beautiful fall sunset. Evan parked his SUV and started his walk up the pathway. It was a chilly evening and the wind did not help matters much as he had forgotten to bring a jacket along. He climbed onto the rock, sat down and stared at the beauty nature provided right in front of him. His thoughts turned to Katie and her big movie night tonight.

The wind picked up, and without a jacket, Evan started to get cold, but the sunset was too beautiful to leave.

He sat alone, staring straight ahead, so deep in his own thoughts he didn't hear the sound of someone climbing upon the rock. A girl stands behind him wearing blue Chuck's, jeans, and a sweater.

"I'm glad I'm not the only one missing my movie tonight," he hears a familiar voice speak. Evan turned his head slowly, hardly believing the voice he heard.

It was Katie. Beautiful Katie, standing there with a smile on her face. Evan stared at her in stunned silence.

"Katie?" he finally stammered. "You're here? How?" he asked.

"Let's just say this last movie squared everything with the studio and we agreed it would be my final film. They're happy, and now....if you'll have me back, I'll finally be happy," Katie said.

Evan didn't even realize he had risen to meet her. He held her tightly in his arms and closed his eyes. This moment could not get any better. *Or could it?* Evan opened his eyes, and what he saw before him once again left him stunned and speechless.

It was his mother. She stood on the summit of Little Round Top watching them and a bright smile shone upon her face.

"You must be freezing," said Katie.

She heard no response.

"Evan, is everything okay?"

"Everything is perfect," he answered, pulling her closer.

He looked back towards the summit and his mother was gone. He knew it wouldn't do any good to look again. She had shown herself just long enough. His mother had let him know she was still watching over him and was now happy for the both of them.

Evan realized Katie was staring at him.

"Did you see someone you know?" she asked.

"I did, but she's gone now," he said with a smile.

Katie wrapped her arms around Evan.

"I've missed you so much. I love you Evan!"

"God, you have no idea how much I've missed you. I love you too Katie!"

They kiss. A golden-red sunset shining upon their faces.

"I'm starting to get cold. Can we go home now," Katie asks.

Still smiling, Evan took her hand and helped her down from the rock. Once they were both on the ground he stopped and stared into Katie's eyes.

"You okay?" she asked once again.

"Your words just hit me. You called my place *home*."

"Well, just to be clear, it's not your place anymore....it's *our* place from now on," said a smiling Katie.

"I can live with that. You know, I feel really bad you missed your movie premiere tonight. Just saying."

"I haven't seen it yet believe it or not, but I wasn't really in the mood to get all dolled up for the red carpet. Cameras in your face, people asking the same questions. Who needs it. I'm in jeans, sneakers and a sweater. I love that I can be me here."

"Aren't you a little bit curious?"

"What are you getting at?"

"You want to?"

"Want to what?"

"Go see your movie silly."

"Now?"

"Yea, why not."

"Do you," Katie asks.

"Sure, I'll just have to close my eyes when dipshit comes on the screen, but yea, sure!"

"You never cease to amaze me, you know that," Katie laughed.

"C'mon, it'll be fun."

They walk to Evan's SUV then drive through town. He finds a parking space and they walk to the theatre where posters of Katie are hanging everywhere. The theatre is packed with people.

Thanks to the paparazzi it was well known throughout the town that Evan and Katie had been seeing each other. It was also well known by all, the heartbreak they each went through, so when they walked into the theatre together, heads turned.

They approach the ticket counter where Evan buys two tickets.

"You want a snack? Some popcorn? Something to drink," Evan asked.

"What's a movie without popcorn and a drink," Katie said with a smile.

They went to the snack counter where Evan orders two drinks, a large popcorn and pays for them. They turn to walk into the theatre. Almost as if on cue, the entire lobby begins to clap for Katie and Evan. Everyone there knew what they had been through and were ecstatic to see them back together and most of all, happy.

This meant the world to Katie as she now knew she was accepted as one of them.

People that were already in the theatre wondering what the commotion was all about began to pour out into the lobby and joined in with the others. Evan and Katie smiled and nodded their heads as they made their way through the cheering crowd towards the theatre to find seats. An usher quickly makes his way to the couple and guides them to the best seats in the house.

Evan and Katie sit and wait as the theatre fills with patrons. Respecting their privacy, nobody bothers them as they take their seats.

"You certainly know how to impress a girl," Katie said with a smile.

"I actually had that planned a few months ago. Cost me twenty bucks a person so I have a lot of books to write now, thanks Katie."

"God how I love the way you can make me laugh. You have no idea how much I've missed that."

"Oh, I'm sorry to hear that."

"I love you Evan Walker."

"I love you too Katie Chambers!"

Evan smiles as Katie rests her head on his shoulder when the lights begin to dim. There is no other place in this world she would rather be than right here, right now. She smiles as the lights fade into darkness.

About the author:

Craig Rupp lives just outside the small, historic town of Gettysburg, Pennsylvania. Besides writing and photography, he can usually be found on a local golf course pursuing his other passion.

Other books by the author:

Love from Beyond and **Karma's Revenge**.

Available at Lulu.com and Amazon

More books coming soon!

Made in the USA
Middletown, DE
12 April 2017